"IF YOU SET OUT TO HUMILIATE ME, YOU'VE SUCCEEDED BRILLIANTLY."

Audra turned her back on him, intending to button her top, when his arms suddenly circled her waist.

"Humiliate you? Is it shameful for you to admit that you might want someone as badly as someone wants you?" He turned her around and cupped her chin with his hand.

Audra looked into the opalescent depths of his eyes and saw raw, unadulterated desire. The intensity of his emotion, which he made no effort to hide or diminish, freed her. She put her arms around his neck and told him in a clear voice, "I want you. I want you to make love to me."

Dear Reader:

As the months go by, we continue to receive word from you that SECOND CHANCE AT LOVE romances are providing you with the kind of romantic entertainment you're looking for. In your letters you've voiced enthusiastic support for SECOND CHANCE AT LOVE, you've shared your thoughts on how personally meaningful the books are, and you've suggested ideas and changes for future books. Although we can't always reply to your letters as quickly as we'd like, please be assured that we appreciate your comments. Your thoughts are all-important to us!

We're glad many of you have come to associate SECOND CHANCE AT LOVE books with our butterfly trademark. We think the butterfly is a perfect symbol of the reaffirmation of life and thrilling new love that SECOND CHANCE AT LOVE heroines and heroes find together in each story. We hope you keep asking for the "butterfly books," and that, when you buy one—whether by a favorite author or a talented new writer—you're sure of a good read. You can trust all SECOND CHANCE AT LOVE books to live up to the high standards of romantic fiction you've come to expect.

So happy reading, and keep your letters coming!

With warm wishes,

Ellen Edwards

Ellen Edwards
SECOND CHANCE AT LOVE
The Berkley/Jove Publishing Group
200 Madison Avenue
New York, NY 10016

Second Chance at Love

SWEET SURRENDER
DIANA MARS

A
**SECOND CHANCE AT LOVE
BOOK**

SWEET SURRENDER

First edition published January 1983

First printing

"Second Chance at Love" and the butterfly emblem are trademarks be-
longing to Jove Publications, Inc.

Printed in the United States of America

Second Chance at Love books are published by
The Berkley/Jove Publishing Group
200 Madison Avenue, New York, NY 10016

SWEET SURRENDER

- 1 -

THE HEAT AND silence of the library tugged on Audra's already frayed nerves. She wondered for the hundredth time when the combined pressures of an assistantship and her own research collided why she had ever decided to pursue a combined degree in anthropology and sociology. Looking about the tomblike periodical section, which belied the jewellike setting of the old campus curving about the shores of one of Minnesota's famed lakes, she smiled wanly. It really was a mine of inspiration for an Egyptologist. When she had her freshman study group hitting the books and cramming the year before, her vivid tales of a transposed Egyptian prince biding his time to appear to them out of the cavernous depths of the stacks had often had them in hysterics.

Unfortunately, she recalled with silent laughter, some pre-med students had overheard her and given her—and her group—a taste of her own medicine. The giant mummy that appeared to them out of the darkness in the silence of the deserted library had all five girls dropping their books and pens and running for their lives. Audra had at first tried to look nonchalant and called back the shrieking girls. But when the mummy made straight for her, she had leaped away screaming, joining her terrified students.

The smile lingered for a moment longer on her lips. But it was quickly chased away by a shadow of pain, as Audra's other memories began crowding in again.

Lifting her jaw in a characteristic gesture of determination, Audra forced the cobwebs of the past away from her mind. It had all happened a long time ago. And until she was able to remember the happy times without the accompanying stabs of hurt, she would just put the past where it belonged and concentrate on the present.

Resolutely ignoring her surroundings, she told herself that she was specializing in urban anthropology, not daydreaming. And if she didn't hurry, she wasn't going to finish her research or have time to correct the exams that lay in haphazard piles on the small table.

An hour later she was again brought to an awareness of her surroundings by the uncomfortable feeling of her light clothes sticking to her moist skin. She was amazed by the amount of research she had completed and was reminded of the unstinting praise from Dr. Phillips, chairman of her department, who had told her that he could really use both her expertise in social science and her way with statistics and computer analysis for the interdisciplinary study to be conducted in beautiful, sunny Puerto Rico.

Just the thought of the location, as well as the value of the experience of working on such a well-focused project with leading members of various fields, made the offer quite tempting. It would mean delaying completion of her own thesis for a few months, but Audra didn't mind. She was tired of being a student. Although she enjoyed learning, she was anxious to go out into the world and leave the protective walls of academia for the less hallowed ones of business.

Audra sighed, and her rounded shoulders slumped dejectedly as she leaned back in the metal chair. She had worn only the vest of her outfit with the full skirt, knowing the matching blouse would be too warm. But the vest, although leaving her shoulders bare, with a ruffly square neckline that almost touched her throat, felt as if it were suffocating her.

Looking about her, Audra noticed that the only other person brave enough—or perhaps desperate enough, with an urgent deadline bearing down on him—to tackle the stacks with a broken air-conditioning system had already left. Audra had seen the man around campus a few times, and he'd always had the preoccupied air of a harried businessman stamped on his tall frame, except those couple of times she'd seen him at the varsity basketball games.

Resisting the urge to follow him and escape the oppressive heat, Audra forced herself to hunt down the last volume she needed to consult before putting all of her information into the computer. Although as an undergraduate Audra had found it quite easy to do research at the university, she was not used to the new system, for the current expansion had subdivided all materials into three categories: books and magazines, microfilm, and computer recall for the most commonly used and often requested information.

Feeling perspiration gather in the valley between her breasts, Audra wiggled delicately but found no immediate relief. Looking about her in exasperation and noticing that the room was quiet and deserted, Audra released the first few buttons. Frustration joined her feelings of discomfort and exhaustion at her failure to locate the elusive book, and after another quick glance, she let the front of her snug ivory vest fall open. Another few minutes of determined searching finally yielded the errant volume. The books, although consecutively numbered and chronologically prepared, had not been replaced in correct order, and she had to suppress the triumphant yell rising in her throat.

Cradling the volume in her right arm, Audra turned around—and promptly encountered a pair of mocking blue-green eyes which effected a leisurely inspection of her figure and returned to her bustline.

"If I had known that going back to college entailed such rewards, especially in this last bastion of dullness, I would have returned sooner." The deep voice rippled with barely contained amusement.

Audra gasped in stunned outrage and felt the betraying warmth creep up her neck and cheeks. Her instinctive reaction was to retreat against the wall of shelves at her back. The coolness of the metal edges brought her a semblance of reason.

"What do you mean by sneaking up on me?" she sputtered indignantly. "I didn't hear you coming up the stairs . . ."

The stranger cut in, "That's because I happen to wear rubber soles. There's nothing more annoying than hearing staccato heels echoing down corridors, wouldn't you agree?" Not waiting for a reply, he continued in a casual tone that assumed her agreement. "I left for dinner a while ago, and when I returned, I noticed your state of abstraction . . . and undress. Being the perfect gentleman I am, I removed myself and retreated to a corner to complete my own research."

"Perfect gentleman, my foot," snorted Audra inelegantly. "You don't know the first thing about being a gentleman or you'd have warned me you were there."

"And you don't know the first thing about men if you think a real man would have stopped you before seeing how far you were prepared to go," the man returned.

"You're — you're disgusting," Audra stuttered, squeezing the book in her hands as if it were his tanned throat.

His quiet laugh flowed over her skin like smooth wine, but the sensuous effect was neutralized when he took a step toward her.

"Stay away from me, you Cro-Magnon moron," Audra stammered, hunching back into the shelves. One part of her mind groaned at her choice of epithet, but even that part fled as he advanced farther, his huge shape blocking out the light from the aisle lamps. Her indignation vanished and was replaced by uncertainty. It appeared her quick temper had gotten her into hot water once again, and she feared that her paleontological adjectives might have put a dent on his obviously highly inflated male ego. Although the man had seemed quite normal and civilized from a distance, she should have known better than to antagonize a man whose civilized veneer paled beneath the onslaught of his animal magnetism.

Wishing she could retract her hastily uttered words, Audra sought to pacify him by appealing to his male vanity. Her mother had always modified adages to fit the many situations Audra continuously got herself into, and Audra vaguely recalled one about catching more flies with honey than vinegar. She was not sure what the recipe was for a stalking panther, which this man resembled, but she gamely added in a sugary tone, "Just a moment ago you told me you were a gentleman. You wouldn't want to ruin your track record, not an intelligent, attractive man like you, now would you?"

Her ploy did not work. He ate the remaining distance between them with two big strides and stood close to Audra, almost touching her. His wide shoulders shaking in silent laughter, he grabbed her chin in a powerful but painless grip and forced her to look up a considerable height at him.

"So now I've progressed from cave dweller to intelligent Homo Sapien, have I?" He lowered his head a fraction, and his gleaming gaze impaled her own. "As for my track record, I'd only be adding to it, not detracting. I always oblige a lady, and from the look of your deliciously unbuttoned vest, you seem to be claiming my attentions."

Audra stared at him in mounting amazement until his last words, softly whispered and accompanied by a burning glance, brought agonizing self-awareness. She hastily tried to rectify her oversight, but his hands prevented her. With incredible speed, her arms were spread-eagled against the shelves, and she noticed the grooves on either side of his mouth deepening.

A tremor, half excitement, half anticipation, shook her body. Audra tried to tell herself that anyone connected with the university and possessing a sense of humor and obvious high I.Q. could not be all bad, then uneasily remembered that Don Juan and Rasputin were reputed to be geniuses with a developed sense of humor. Her throat constricted. Her whole body seemed one numb entity as she watched his mouth complete its downward arc with maddening slowness. At the moment of contact, another shudder convulsed her body, but this time of a different sort.

As his kiss deepened and he tried to part her lips, Audra struggled, attempting to fight the strange effect he had on her senses as well as his encroaching mouth. She tried to free her arms and at the same time, recalling isolated bits on the art of self-defense, she moved her knee upward at a sharp angle, intending to connect it with his groin. Instead, she met a solid weight which seemed to crush her knee as his own leg blocked her offense with disgustingly quick defense, and a groan of pain and surprise escaped her lips.

Raising his head, he looked at her with mocking sympathy. "Tut, tut, no way for a lady to act. Now, we both know what you'd really like to do. If I free your hands, will you behave sensibly?"

At her eager nod, he released her arms and stepped back, allowing her breathing space. Straightening her back, which Audra was convinced would forever bear the imprints of the shelves, she tossed her hair away from her face and directed a dazzling smile at the stranger.

"You are so right," she said sweetly. "I must act sensibly." She aimed a hard kick at his shin and an elbow at his stomach. Although not able to stop her kick, the stranger easily evaded her elbow with one smooth turn of his upper body, and Audra found herself with both hands held securely behind her back by one of his, her body pressed again to the shelves.

"Now I know he's read the same article," she muttered, struggling ineffectually but stubbornly to disengage her arms.

Audra heard the low-pitched chuckle and looked at the stranger as if doubting his mental capacity.

"There is nothing funny about this," she enunciated with commendable dignity under the circumstances.

"That is one thing we seem to agree on," the man drawled, a wide smile relieving the harsh, lean planes of his tanned face. "It has never taken me this long to secure a response."

"There you have it," Audra exclaimed eagerly. "It just shows how incompatible we are."

"I intend to prove quite differently," he said with a confident grin. "Anyone who starts disrobing in a library must be very hot-blooded, a woman after my own heart."

"You conceited gorilla!" cried a frustrated Audra. "I was not doing a strip-tease, and if I am after your heart, my own use for it would be to cut it into thin strips. If there is a heart to cut out."

Her outburst had no effect on him except to make his smile even wider. "Such a bloodthirsty woman! Had I more time, I'd continue our debate, but unfortunately duty calls." Wicked lights danced in the blue-green eyes scorching Audra.

"Oh don't let me keep you," Audra said quickly. "I wouldn't want..."

But her sentence was never finished, as his mouth swooped down and this time successfully penetrated her defenses. His tongue separated her lips and explored the roof of her mouth. Audra moaned and tried to evade his velvet invasion, but his frontal attack made it impossible.

When she began to choke for air, her tormentor asked

in a mocking whisper, "Is that a new way of showing sexual arousal? Because if it is, I must tell you it needs working on."

Before she could retort, he kissed her again, and this time, when the essence of his kiss manifested itself on her taste buds, she found her body turned traitor. The heat of his body was burning her skin, the muskiness of his male scent was a potent drug to her senses. Audra was conscious with every fiber of her being of the muscular hardness of his body, the strength of his thighs locking hers.

She felt light-headed from the reeling sensations assaulting her wavering equilibrium. When she pushed him away, he accommodated and removed his mouth—temporarily. But before Audra could resume her normal breathing, his warm lips sought the sensitive hollow at the base of her neck, and she uttered a faint moan. His free hand gently stroked her body, molding her breast briefly as it moved upward from her waist, before settling on one smooth, round shoulder.

The intimate caress over her soft flesh was igniting new sensations that fevered her racing pulse. His lips trailed kisses in a fiery path down her neck, shoulders, then moved upward again, claiming her lips in a soul-destroying kiss. This time Audra could not restrain herself and responded ardently to his kiss, forgetting the fact that he was still basically a stranger, that she didn't even know his name.

The dizzying waves came again and excitement thundered through her veins as the melting sensation that spread through her affected her legs, which could no longer support her. Her helplessness terrified her, and ashamed of her submission and capitulation, Audra rebelled with frenzied fury. Her efforts seemed fruitless for a long moment, and then her captor stiffened and, visibly forcing himself to relax, slowly let her go.

He looked bemusedly down at Audra and for a while was at a loss for words. Audra could not utter a single syllable; her mind was a blank. Her eyes examined his strong defined features as if memorizing them for all time. She noticed how his black hair fell in a stubborn wave over his wide forehead, how his long lashes veiled his expression, the firm mouth, his arrogantly chiseled chin.

"Well, kitten, we sure ignited like a dry forest, didn't we?" he rasped in a self-mocking tone. He seemed to expect some sort of response, and when none was forthcoming, gently raised her chin so she would be forced to look into his smoldering gaze.

The sudden touch broke the spell which had immobilized Audra. She jerked her chin away and stepped back hastily to put as much distance as possible between them.

"Don't you dare touch me again," Audra cried. "If you lay a hand on me again, I swear I'll . . ."

"You'll what?"

Audra's eyes flew to his at the gentle words, seeking signs of mockery in his eyes, his face. But there was none to be found.

She faltered in confusion and suddenly felt the need to explain to the stranger. She did not understand her compulsion, but told herself she would analyze it later. Squaring her shoulders and holding her vest closed with shaking hands, Audra began uncertainly. "I realize I might appear foolish or provocative to you by opening my top, but there's usually no one here at this time, especially now that they're renovating and expanding the library, and most materials are at the south end. Besides, I did check . . ."

"I know. I saw your quick look around."

"Then why? Why would you ever . . ." Audra found herself unable to continue, unable to comprehend his actions.

"Because I'd been observing you for two hours while doing my own research. When I took a dinner break, I fully intended to dismiss from my mind a delectable soft body with a face to match, and found instead the image of large green eyes and enticing curves embedded in my brain."

"But I didn't see you," Audra said weakly.

"You were too lost in those dusty volumes. And besides, I didn't intend for you to notice me," the stranger said with an arrogance which passed unnoticed by Audra for the moment. "I fully expected you to be gone when I returned." A slow smile started at the corners of the sensuous male mouth and spread to his blue-green eyes. "When I came back and saw you there, still tackling those horrendous books, I knew I could not resist approaching you." The corners of his eyes crinkled in devilish amusement as he added softly, "But I didn't know you'd make it so easy."

Audra had been listening in a mesmerized state, her body still climbing down from long-forgotten feelings, her mind lulled by the seductive timbre of the deep voice and the hypnotic quality of the opalescent eyes. But his last words lashed at her sluggish mind, and his arrogance stung. She reminded herself that she had cause to feel insulted by him. Even if she had fully responded at the end, that still did not excuse his offensive behavior. And it certainly did not mean that she was ready to fall at his feet like ripe fruit. The more she thought about it, the more incensed Audra became.

Gathering her belongings at top speed, Audra fixed a cold stare on him and told him haughtily, "You really have nerve!"

"And flesh and blood and muscles. Want to feel?" he retorted outrageously, and Audra gaped at him for a moment before turning away.

Throwing her books into her carry-all with renewed outrage, Audra picked up her purse and slung it over her shoulder. Warily eyeing the tall figure in blue shirt and slacks blocking her exit, Audra carefully kept her distance as she edged toward the stairs.

Convinced he would pounce on her at the last minute, Audra nearly jumped out of her skin when he moved to give her more room to pass. His odiously knowing smile told Audra he was aware of the thoughts running through her mind. She was halfway to the metal staircase when his deep voice reached her once more. "By the way, my name is Grant Williams."

Audra half ran the remaining distance, and when on the first step, knowing herself safe even in the unlikely event he gave chase, she turned around and quite distinctly said, "Go to hell!"

Expecting anger on his part, or at least displeasure, Audra was shocked at the sight of him throwing his head back in gusty laughter. Knowing he had won the last round also, Audra hurried down the metal steps in impotent fury. Only when she reached the main floor did she temper the sound of her high-heeled sandals, still wishing it was not the floor but Grant Williams's equally hard head she was stomping on.

- 2 -

AN HOUR LATER, Audra approached the librarians' station, centrally located in the newly renovated section of the library. She had stopped by the ladies' room to restore order to her hair and clothes and had finished her research in the glass-enclosed lounge overlooking the lake. The sight of its dark blue waters surrounding the green lawns of the campus at sunset soothed her. It had always held that power for her, ever since Jimmy's death, when she had fiercely immersed herself in her studies. She had found pleasure in the muted conversations of fellow students and in watching the play of the seasons on the lake's chameleon surface, turning it now a sapphire blue, now a turbulent gray, or more often covering it with a sparkling coat of white, an abundant commodity in southeastern Minnesota.

Mona Farwell was at her station, her petite figure lost behind the huge desk and surrounding reference shelves. Audra saw she was patiently explaining some of the finer

13

points of the Dewey system to a couple of bewildered looking students.

Audra put the heavy volume on top of the neat desk and leaned against a corner of it while she waited for her friend to complete her explanation.

"Hi, Audra. Be right with you." Mona smiled as she finished giving instructions to the two freshmen. "Whew, what a day! Not only do I get to fill in for Frank and postpone my crucial date with Steve, but I've been deluged with questions all day. I've been thinking of providing a weekly class titled 'How to use your college library.' Some of these questions are constantly recurring and quite basic."

"Why don't you? Sounds like a great idea," concurred Audra. "My own introduction was a quickie tour conducted during an English class," she recalled. "Hardly enlightening."

"I might just do it if I get proper backing. And how did your research go, Audra? Did you have an exciting time in your favorite spot?" asked Mona teasingly, knowing Audra's abhorrence of the stacks.

Audra laughed shakily at her friend's unknowingly accurate description. "Well, I've certainly earned a few days off." Then, pointing to the book on Mona's desk, she asked, "Could I leave this with you today? I'm in kind of a rush." She didn't tell her friend that wild horses could not have dragged her back to the stacks. "I still have to pack when I get home." At Mona's nod, Audra smiled her thanks and asked, "Sure you don't want to come along?"

"Me, roughing it?" Mona unconsciously smoothed her perfect blond chignon. "You know I'd rather dance till all hours of the morning. No fresh air, but plenty of exercise." Picking up the phone, she quickly jotted down the question, told the caller she would have the answer in fifteen minutes, and turned back to Audra. "When are you leaving?"

"Tomorrow morning, as early as I can manage it. One of my students will be entering my research in the social science computer. He's doing it for a project, and it will free me from trying to get access to it every night."

"That bad?" commiserated Mona.

Audra nodded her response and began picking up her purse and canvas bag. "They really need another one, but financing is tight right now. Well, I'd better be going."

Mona handed the book Audra had been using to the library clerk and got up to hug Audra. "I really don't see how you can want to vacation in solitary splendor, but I guess it takes all kinds." Mona's grin took the sting out of her words. "Take care of yourself."

"I'll only be gone for a few days, and it's just a couple of hundred miles away, for heaven's sake," Audra protested, but she was secretly touched by Mona's concern.

"I still don't like to think of you going camping alone. But if you do meet a handsome forest ranger, make sure he finds a friend for me," Mona joked.

"I will, and I'll send him straight to Steve." Aware that Mona's boyfriend would have something to say about that, Audra laughed at the tiny fist Mona raised in her direction.

Opening her bags for the check-out clerk's inspection, she knew Mona would be busy researching the telephone caller's question, so she did not turn around to wave goodbye and went out into the warm, star-filled night.

* * *

The insistent ringing of the phone brought a wet, muttering Audra out of the bathroom. Holding the huge green towel about her with one hand, she picked up the white receiver with the other. Her "Hello" sounded less than gracious, and it received a familiar chuckle in response.

Her skin prickling, Audra tried to sound calm. She would need her wits to deal with the man. "How did you get my number?"

"Oh, Mona was most accommodating. She even gave me your address when she found out I had to return some of your notes," Grant said, "but I didn't think you would have calmed down enough to let me in. Seems I was right," he added softly, and Audra could envision the smile reflected in his voice. He had made an indelible impression on her, and she was not at all pleased.

"You were certainly right. For once," she could not resist adding, because the fact that he had seemed to read her character so well was not encouraging.

Then the rest of his statement sank in. "What notes?"

"You and I both know there aren't any notes, but Mona didn't. She thanked me quite profusely on your behalf, knowing you would be anxious to give them to your students before you left."

"You really are despicable," Audra said in a voice filled with feeling.

"Now, now. It's incredible, the number of adjectives you have at your command to describe me. Dare I hope I've made an impression on you?" Audra knew he was silently laughing at her, as he seemed to have been doing since he'd met her only that afternoon. The insufferable boor! She felt fury rush through her veins in an unwelcome return of feeling. Audra had liked the pleasant numbness she had experienced for the past three years and did not thank Grant for the gamut of emotions he had been able to rouse in her in only a few hours.

"Mr. Williams," she intoned severely, ignoring the fact that in her mind he was already Grant, "I don't know why you're going out of your way to torment me . . ."

"Don't you?" he cut in smoothly.

". . . and furthermore, I couldn't care less. I do know I did not give you my phone number, and it would have been a cold day in hell before you ever got it from me . . ."

"I gathered as much," he interrupted once more, leaving her with the uneasy sensation he was not only referring to the phone number.

"I don't even know how Mona could show so little common sense, and I'll have a word with her when I get back. But let me tell you, Mr. Williams, your dubious charm will not work on me, and if you ever—but ever—dare call me again at this number, I not only will have it changed, but I will report you to the police."

Audra ran out of breath as well as words, and Grant calmly stepped in. "First things first, Audra. If you were not such a scared little hypocrite, you would know that there is more than dubious charm involved. And believe me, honey, it's mutual." Audra was incensed at his use of her first name, and even more so at his calling her "honey," but he did not give her a chance to speak. "Second, don't be upset at Mona. I've been in the library before and have had the opportunity to meet Mona on other occasions. Besides which, I am a personal friend of the dean's and have contributed a substantial portion toward the restoration of the library, a project long over-due."

It took a few seconds for Audra to assimilate the astonishing information, but her agile mind quickly found a loophole. "You say you donated to the library reno-vation. But there is no record of any Williams . . ."

"The donation was made under my company's name."

Audra digested this further revelation slowly, but she had no doubt Grant Williams was telling the truth. For some reason she knew that Grant would never call at-tention to himself, and his overwhelming self-assurance precluded any idle boasts or self-aggrandizement.

Still, the information, although surprising, was not the real issue, and she told him so. "I would rather forget we ever met, and I would appreciate your throwing my number away." She hated sounding so polite but knew that antagonizing Grant Williams would never get her anywhere. She sighed at the realization that their heated, vibrant encounter in the library had also revealed certain aspects of his personality to her.

"I know you would, Audra," Grant told her gently, as if humoring a child. "But after this afternoon, you should know it's impossible." Audra was quite prepared to take issue with his assumption, but he forestalled her, asking quite casually, "And where are you off to?"

He asked his question so casually that Audra almost answered before she caught herself. About to say flip-pantly, "None of your business," she decided to throw him off the scent and lied quite cheerfully, "To my par-ents. I haven't seen them in quite a while." That much of it was true, at least.

The silence that greeted her answer made Audra shift

nervously on the sofa, and his next words made her jump off it. "Well then, I won't keep you up much longer. I'll wait until you get back to take you out to dinner. When *are* you coming back, and what kind of food do you prefer, so I can make the necessary reservations?"

Picking up the towel which had slid off her body with her violent movement, Audra answered heatedly, "My preferences are my own affair, and so is the date of my return. Good night, Mr. Williams!" Slamming down the receiver gave her some satisfaction, but not nearly enough. Audra hoped it had broken his eardrums, but she had the unhappy feeling they were as unbreakable as his ego.

Her hair received its most vigorous washing in years, and when Audra finally finished towel-drying it in front of her small brick fireplace, it gleamed in golden-brown glory.

She combed it carefully into its inward cut, liking the pageboy hairdo because it looked feminine without much work. Although Audra used to wear it past her shoulders and had curled it religiously as a teenager, nowadays she found she barely had time to take a shower in the mornings. Her days of leisure were gone, especially now that she was working on a combined major. But Audra found she enjoyed her hectic lifestyle. Although at first it had been a panacea, it had become a lot more. She liked the feeling of independence it gave her, the sense of accomplishment. Professional maturity brought its own rewards.

Looking down into the coral flames, Audra found two blue-green eyes impinged in the swaying lights. She realized now that what had at first shocked her into awareness of Grant was his unusual eyes, which were identical in color to Jimmy's. She remembered how she used to tease her husband, telling him his eyes were prettier than hers. Those were the carefree days when she had almost dyed her hair black after Jimmy had retorted that her green eyes were the prettiest he'd ever seen, almond-shaped like those of Cleopatra.

Audra shook her head free of her memories but found it more difficult to tear loose from the power of those eyes whose color was the only similarity to Jimmy. Grant's hair was black, where Jimmy's had been blond; he was tall and muscular, where Jimmy had been of slender build. But by far the most noticeable difference was in personality. Jimmy had been easygoing, trusting, and non-aggressive. Grant Williams was too sure of himself, cynical, and much too disturbing. He truly did belong in the caves of prehistory, where Audra impatiently consigned him and his power to invade her mind at will.

Knowing she needed activity to keep her from constantly reliving her meeting and conversation with Grant—a man she had decided to ignore and forget—Audra got up, and retying her black-and-jade kimono around her slender waist, headed toward the kitchen area. Her bare feet sank into the cream shag, and she looked around her living-dining room combination with a mixture of pride and warmth. It was not much—she had painted the walls salmon pink herself and had refurbished her secondhand furniture on weekends—but it was all hers and comfortably reflected her personality.

Leaning against the orange counter while sipping her cocoa, Audra wiggled her toes at the cool pleasure of the parquet tile. Her lips curved into a smile of satisfaction at the thought of the wrath Grant would experience when he tried to contact her over the next few days. Even if he did attempt to find out her parents' number from

Mona, she would not be there. And if Mona was her predictable self and tried a spot of matchmaking by telling him her destination, she would already be in Devil's Lake by then, and he would not know in which camping site to find her.

Rinsing the mug and small pan she'd used to heat the milk, Audra gave the counter one last wipe before leaving the tiny orange and white kitchen. She'd already packed some potato chips and fruit to munch on during the trip, though she would be stopping for a late breakfast in Wisconsin. Audra enjoyed traveling early in the morning, when the roads were clear and the highways seemed to stretch for miles and miles just for her. Getting caught in morning rush-hour traffic would put her behind an hour or more, and that was time she could spend swimming or horseback riding in clean country air.

Setting her alarm clock for four o'clock, Audra noticed it was almost midnight. Shrugging, she told herself she could catch up on her much needed rest that evening. She was always surprised at how much better she seemed to sleep when she didn't have the so-called modern conveniences.

The last thought on her mind as she snuggled under the mint green sheets was that she wished she could be a fly on the wall when Grant Williams found out she was not available. It would at least repay her somewhat for his cavalier treatment of her and his unmitigated gall and conceit.

- 3 -

AUDRA QUICKLY DETERMINED she would be first in line
to board the ferry and smiled as she recalled how it had
always seemed so important to be first when she'd come
with her parents on their traditional Labor Day camping
trips. More often than not, they had been sandwiched
between other cars, and being first had always seemed
a happy portend to her.

She picked up her purse from the vinyl seat, and
although she really liked the combination of scarlet ex-
terior and black interior on her Malibu, on hot days like
this Audra wished her car was a frigid, all-white model.

Feeling thirsty and in need of some quick energy—
her breakfast had evaporated along with the traces of rain
she'd noticed when first entering Wisconsin—Audra
headed slowly for the refreshment stand. She ordered an
orange drink and looked longingly toward the ferry making its snail's-pace return trip. Shaking her head at her
own kidlike anticipation, Audra reflected she had not

outgrown her tendency toward impatience. As a child she'd always wanted to go out there and push it, because it was so unfair that it took forever to wait for it and yet the trip across the wide body of water seemed to be accomplished in only a few seconds.

As she stood under the welcome shade of the awning sipping her drink, Audra looked longingly at the vanilla sugar cone a child of about five was delightfully demolishing.

"Hot day, isn't it?" Audra commented to the young mother who was holding a baby on her left arm while trying to pay for her snacks with her heavily pursed right hand.

"It sure is," agreed the beleaguered mother. "It's times like this when I feel being an octopus would be a definite advantage."

Putting down her drink on the spotless counter, Audra said, "Here, why don't you let me hold your baby for a while? And you can get yourself something to drink." Audra lifted the child out of the woman's tired arms.

"Thank you so much!" The woman smiled gratefully. "This trip has been something of an ordeal, what with three children . . ."

"Three children?" repeated Audra, surprised.

The woman nodded her blond head. "My oldest, Kevin, is standing next to his father, Kevin Senior."

Audra looked in the direction the woman had pointed and spotted a boy of about eight standing near a red-haired man who was talking to some other men. The boy seemed a small replica of the father. Audra smiled down at the tiny bundle in her arms, and solemn big blue eyes peeped back at her.

The woman must have read her mind, because she

smiled also and said, "Yes, Erin takes after me. And a lucky thing too. Ryan and Kevin are typical green-eyed redheads, like their father. They can take the 'carrottop' teasing a lot better than girls can."

"Oh, I don't know about that," Audra said in a doubtful tone. "I think red hair is quite lovely and unusual."

"Yes, but with a face full of freckles?" At this, Ryan, who looked quite disreputable after finishing his ice cream and managing to transfer a lot of it to nose and chin, made a face. "See what I mean?" His mother grinned.

Audra laughed, and the baby began to make small gurgling sounds, diverting their attention. The baby's hair was a faint blond down, and Audra remarked on it, after making answering sounds to baby Erin, which caused tiny dimples to appear on the chubby pink cheeks.

"She's a regular bowling ball," the woman said. "But my mom tells me I was too; it seems to run in the family."

"Your daughter *is* an adorable bundle," laughed Audra and Erin smiled on cue, as if appreciating the compliment.

"Oh, here comes the ferry now. Thank you so much again for your help," said the woman, hurriedly finishing her Coke.

"Don't mention it. It was a pleasure."

"By the way, I noticed your camping gear on the luggage rack. Are you by any chance going to Devil's Lake?" asked the woman, as she tried to attract her husband's attention away from what appeared a very lively discussion.

"Yes, I am. Are you headed there yourself?" Audra inquired as she transferred her precious charge to the mother.

"Yes. We've come all the way from Indianapolis. But

with a large family, we thought it'd be cheaper to camp, and the children could get some fresh air and also manage to get in the attractions at Baraboo and Wisconsin Dells." She pulled at the baby's tiny fist that was playing tug-of-war with its mother's blond curls.

"Well, you won't be sorry," assured Audra. "You'll find it's well worth the long trip."

"By the way," the woman said, extending her right hand, "my name's Heather Donahue. Perhaps we'll see each other on the grounds."

Audra reciprocated the greeting and added, "We're bound to meet each other." Throwing the empty cup into the garbage can nearby, Audra waved goodbye to Heather and strode back to her car, breathing deeply of the rain-washed air.

Taking one last look at the lumbering carrier, Audra noticed it had been recently repainted, the resplendent silver a vivid contrast to turquoise waters and azure firmament. Feeling the always new thrill at the sight of the ferry separating the clear waters into two foamy waves, Audra got in just as the signal to embark sounded. She directed her wheels onto the guiding planks until she felt her bumper touch the metal in front of her. After automatically applying the manual brakes, Audra left the stuffiness of her car, thinking that the rain had not done much to cool this part of Wisconsin. The temperature was as scorching here as it had been back in Minnesota, almost two hundred miles away.

As she leaned against the railing, watching the teasing ebb and flow upon the emerald banks, Audra barely heard the clunking sounds of other cars climbing aboard. She was too concerned with enjoying the highlight of her trip and threw her head back to receive fully the whipping breeze and hot sunlight on her face. Several people left their cars and crowded the sides, flanking her, their excited chatter failing to penetrate her consciousness.

Hearing heavy footsteps approaching her spot and thinking absently that it was someone switching sides to enjoy another section of the view, Audra moved a bit to her right to give extra room. But the voice that caressed her ear almost had her somersaulting into the Wisconsin River.

"Fancy meeting you here. Small world, isn't it?" The clichés rolled smoothly from the man she'd hoped never to meet again.

Audra whipped around to face him, her ponytail stinging her face from the force of the turn. She couldn't believe—didn't want to believe—that Grant was really standing in front of her.

"What are you doing here?" To her dismay, her voice came out husky instead of accusingly cold as she'd intended.

Grant shrugged his wide shoulders, stretching the navy knit to its limit. "Free country, isn't it? Besides, although I live quite close to the dells, I've never sampled the attractions." Running his eyes appreciatively over her white shorts and red halter top, he added wickedly, "It's the old story of not taking advantage of what's near."

Despite herself, Audra felt her heart beat a rapid tattoo, and it had nothing to do with the fright he'd given her. Grant's hair was a lustrous ebony in the sunlight, his eyes a blue-green that matched the disturbed river depths, and his smile dazzlingly white against his deep tan. Her eyes involuntarily danced over his tall, broad physique, the sleek muscled arms revealed by the short-sleeved shirt, the flat stomach, the long legs tightly encased in worn blue jeans. She noticed he was wearing boots, which accounted for the fact that she'd heard his approach this time.

As she looked up again and saw his amusement at her unsubtle scrutiny, she felt a violent blush stain her cheeks and spoke rapidly, feeling extremely flustered.

"I thought you hated loud shoes," she said, and could have kicked herself when his smile deepened the laugh lines that carved his lean cheeks.

"No, I don't hate loud shoes," he denied with laughter evident in his voice. "I merely dislike things out of place, such as disturbingly noisy heels in the quiet of a library."

"So according to you, women should wear gym shoes with their fancy slacks outfits or dresses?" Audra wondered why she was letting herself take part in such a ridiculous discussion.

"Not at all. I like women," Audra squirmed as his gaze ran expertly over her heated body once more, "to dress for the occasion. You must admit that many young girls are not academically minded and use those heels with extreme effectiveness in order to get noticed."

Audra knew him to be right, since she'd observed quite a few girls doing exactly that—including herself as an undergraduate—but nothing in the world would make her admit it.

"Then I suggest you and those men so greatly bothered by a little noise start up a collection and get every library fitted with wall-to-wall carpeting," she said sweetly. Shifting position, Audra moved back a bit, finding it a strain to look up into his eyes from her own five feet five without the advantage of high heels. She wished she'd worn her open-heeled wedgies instead of these confidence-draining sneakers.

"I would if I had to spend a large amount of time in libraries. But it's been a long time since I've had to use libraries on a constant basis," he answered, raking his wind-ruffled hair with impatient fingers.

"I can well believe that," Audra muttered. Although she tried to look at him with disdain, it was hard to fake indifference when confronted with his powerful virility.

To her surprise, he smiled at her dig. "Those cat eyes sure do go well with your disposition, Audra," he said mockingly, riling her with his implication and his free use of her first name.

About to tell him she'd given him no leave to call her by her first name, Audra desisted, deciding to pursue the major issue.

"How did you find out I'd be here?" she asked him coolly, pushing down the anger that threatened to erupt.

"Lucky guess, I suppose," he drawled, exposing those very white teeth Audra privately thought akin to a shark's. So much for her fly on the wall fantasy. Right now she felt more like fish bait.

"You asked Mona," she accused, staring into the brilliant eyes as if to drag the truth from them. "And you let me believe you didn't know where I was going." To think he'd let her make a complete fool out of herself. Oh, the man had a lot to answer for!

Grant leaned back on his elbows against the railing, and his sudden reduction in height relieved the crick in Audra's neck. "Would you have come here if I'd let on I was aware of your destination?" As her silence spoke volumes, he continued gently, "Mona volunteered the information. She told me how you had been working so

hard teaching and researching and how you really deserved this break before you collapsed."

Audra gritted her teeth, thinking that if anything were
to cause her undue demise, it would be the prime male
specimen relaxing inches away from her and glancing at
her with a thoroughness which left no territory uncharted.
When his eyes met hers again, they indicated he'd seen
no major damage so far. Audra burned inside and out
and longed to tell him what she thought of his predatory
tactics.

Instead, she decided to find out how much he knew
and where he would be staying. Then she'd do her
damnedest to be out of that vicinity.

"So you decided to explore, so to speak, these wonderful spots, which, lovely though they may be, have
been here for hundreds of years and doubtless will be
around for another few hundred? Why, Mr. Williams?
Why here, and why now?" Although it did nothing to
preserve the indifferent attitude she was trying to assume,
she could not resist the question.

"Explore." He rolled the word around his tongue in
a way Audra considered positively indecent, and those
devilish glints she'd first seen the night before in his
blue-green eyes became more pronounced in the intense
summer light. "That's exactly the right word for what
I'm planning." He nodded his head slowly, a black lock
of hair sliding closer to a thickly etched eyebrow. "You
sure do have a way with words."

"I can't say I return the compliment," Audra retorted
tartly. Then, remembering she was trying to procure information, she forced lightness into her tone. "You'll be
staying at one of the camping sites around here?"

Her attempt at casualness obviously failed. His eyes

acquired that familiarly mocking expression, although his voice remained bland. "I doubt it. I'm sure most of the camping sites will be full up. Mona mentioned you'd made reservations a few months ago."

"How nice of Mona," Audra said, not bothering to keep the sarcasm out of her voice now. She wondered uneasily just how much Mona had told him. At this rate, he'd even know what she'd looked like as a baby. A picture her father had snapped of her in her bath at age two rose to her mind, and Audra felt embarrassment and irritation flood her in equal force at the thought of Grant even coming close to such a picture.

Damn him! She bit her lip savagely, knowing he was playing cat-and-mouse with her and outwitting her at every turn. Grant knew she wanted to find out where he'd be staying. Frustrated, she chose to attack.

"So you decided to follow me."

"Follow you?" Grant repeated innocently. "Not at all. I merely concluded I was overdue for a vacation, and your plans sounded most sensible."

Audra stared at him. The fingers of her right hand were numb from gripping the railing so hard, and she could not wait to leave. She saw they were approaching the shore and heaved an inner sigh of relief.

"Isn't it a bit coincidental that we're both on the ferry at the same time?"

Grant looked over the neat row of cars. "Not really. I got this particular crossing through sheer luck. I'm twelfth in line." Audra followed his gaze and saw a light blue Cadillac at the end of the third row.

"So you admit that your being here has nothing whatsoever to do with me." There, she had him, Audra thought triumphantly. Now she'd ask him where he was staying, offer him advice on sightseeing attractions, and make sure she stayed out of his way.

Grant straightened and the animal movement brought him in such close contact that Audra stepped back, bumping into a car. Grant's arms snaked out and around her waist with ease. "I wouldn't say that either," he drawled with maddening ease. "I was fully expecting to meet you *sometime* today, but this early rendezvous is a bonus."

Audra marveled, not sure whether to laugh or cry, "And you admit it so nonchalantly."

"Of course. Truthfulness is another of my many virtues," he told her with another flash of white teeth before releasing her and walking toward his car. Audra was stupefied by his determination, but she couldn't keep her eyes off his retreating form or still her racing heart.

"I don't suppose you would consider making things easier and telling me the number of your lot?" he called out before getting into his car.

Audra's answer was to practically dive into her car and slam the door shut out of embarrassment.

As she waited irritably for the front of the ferry to flap down, Audra thought, so much for good omens. She had not even been aware of the ride she had so looked forward to. And she feared for her peace of mind, and the rest of her vacation as well.

Audra turned left as soon as she disembarked and drove thoughtfully through the quaint town with its quiet, tree-bordered residential streets and spacious houses. She wished she could afford to keep a home here, or at least a cottage on one of the lakes. Maybe if she were careful enough she could buy a small cottage in a few years.

Although Audra really enjoyed city living, she had been looking forward to a break from the city on weekends. And Lodi, where the many springs in the area had once turned grist mills, seemed just the place. It had a peaceful uniqueness which was not spoiled by the many visitors who camped at nearby Devil's Lake, and the state's last ferry was an added treat to look forward to on a Friday.

Smiling and shaking her head at plans which might never be realized, Audra turned west at the intersection and felt her tension ease as she sighted the road guarded by a thick profusion of trees on one side and blunt cliff on the other. The steep slope emptied her mind of the previous interlude as it forced her to concentrate fully on her driving. Since thrill-seeking motorcyclists sometimes roared down simultaneously with cars on a road barely wide enough to accommodate two cars, Audra was doubly careful.

The sharp curves finally gave way to a flat stretch of land, and the registration office soon came into view, as well as the large Devil's Lake, which glinted with sapphire crystals in the strong sunlight. She parked her car between others also sporting out-of-state license plates and went into the office to collect her map and confirm her reservation.

Audra stepped back to admire her handiwork. Her gold-colored tent—a present from her parents—was up and seemed secure enough. Driving the pegs into the ground to necessary depth was the hardest part of putting up the large tent, but she had discovered after one extremely stormy night that it was essential.

She had devoted extra time to making sure the sides of the cabin tent were taut enough, and the added effort had paid off. Before setting up camp Audra had gone to purchase logs for her campfire and had also stocked up temporarily with some provisions from the merchandise store at the base of the park.

Before sweeping the inside of the tent and inflating her mattress, Audra decided to get a drink. The interior was crawling with daddy longlegs—spiders with tiny bodies and tremendously long, skinny legs—and the ever present ants. She would need to clear her cozy canvas home of its uninvited inhabitants before emptying her trunk and transferring her belongings inside. Thinking of the refreshing swim she would have in a little while, Audra sipped the grapefruit juice slowly, letting the cold, tangy taste revive her parched mouth.

Audra heard a car pull up behind her and turned to explain that the lot was already taken. The words died in her throat as she saw Grant get out of his car, imparting her small parcel of earth, trees, and flowers with electricity. His hair was still wet from a recent shower, and he'd changed into another pair of jeans and a short-sleeved white shirt. His boots crunched on the dirt as he made his way slowly to her side, his eyes taking in her hot face and dusty jeans and T-shirt. Audra pulled nervously at her pink top, which after repeated washings tended to ride up and hug her curves like a second skin.

"You never give up, do you, Grant?" Audra asked in bitter defeat.

"Did you really expect me to, Audra?" he asked softly. "Or even want me to?"

Audra's mouth tightened, and she wished she could answer with a resounding negative. But she knew the moment she'd seen him that, despite her repeated denunciations, she could never be the victor in the war of desire against Grant. She'd been unconsciously waiting for him, and while consciously she knew it was a madness, that didn't help cancel the light, airy feeling she'd experienced at knowing he'd driven through the camping grounds until he had located her car. And her.

Grant came closer and leaned forward, and Audra instinctively backed away, thinking he was going to kiss her. But Grant gripped her chin and, tilting it, licked her upper lip free of its beads of moisture. "Hmmmm, you taste good," he murmured. "Sweet and salty all at once."

Audra pulled away, shocked, even more so than if he'd tried to caress her in public.

His eyes took in her round, dazed ones, and he smiled gently. "Don't you know I like everything about you, sweetheart? Even your disheveled appearance and hard-earned perspiration?"

His endearment turned her stomach to the consistency of melted butter, and Audra raised a trembling hand to her tangled hair, the wet tendrils curled wildly about her face as they fought the confining pink hair band. Swallowing past the tight ring about her throat, she tried again. "Grant," she managed hoarsely, "I realize you are a mature man and have doubtless used love words many times before in your relationships with women without a second thought. But I would appreciate it if you wouldn't use them so facilely with me. My husband..." she swallowed again convulsively, "...he used to say them all the time, and although he's been dead three years... well, I just... I guess I just don't..."

Grant nodded, sobering instantly. "All right, Audra. I'll try to keep from calling you by anything but your first name. But only if you promise not to bombard me with that arsenal of adjectives you carry around with you."

Audra smiled weakly in response to the gentle teasing, but the smile fled when she realized she'd tacitly arrived at a decision. Her uneasiness increased when he told her softly, "But you have to realize, Audra, that it won't be easy. I seldom call women by other than their given names, but around you, they just pop up naturally." Rather than reassure her, his obvious sincerity increased her tension. "And I also promise to use restraint in other matters too," he added gravely, but she noticed the devilish glint lurking behind the mocking seriousness in his eyes and couldn't help the tremulous smile that curved her lips.

"I'll hold you to that promise," she threatened, and as she watched him walk to his car, she felt the tension draining from her body.

"Would you like to go into town for dinner?" he asked as he opened the door.

Audra sighed, knowing that this was the time to tell him she didn't want to see him, that if he didn't leave her alone she'd be forced to go home. But Grant had accomplished his mission too well. He'd overwhelmed her senses to the point where making a totally rational decision was no longer possible. So she said instead, "No. I'm too tired to dress up. I'd like to have an early dinner and take it easy tonight."

Grant nodded. "See you at seven, then. I'll bring some wine." His glance caressed her in that all-encompassing way she was almost growing accustomed to. His eyes seemed to transmit hungry sensual waves that bound her to him, and her breathing quickened in response. Then he was leaving, and although her campsite seemed suddenly lonely, she welcomed the momentary respite from his forceful masculinity. She needed time to think.

- *4* -

BY THE TIME Grant returned that evening, Audra had armored herself in a thick, long-sleeved shirt, to ward off the chills of the early summer night, and—she hoped—a cool, calm, and collected attitude. She'd decided that she might as well take advantage of Grant's exciting company, reflecting ruefully that it had not taken her long to convince herself of that.

She supposed she should be grateful to live again, to feel really alive once more. But Grant might not be the man she should be trying her wings on. He was too compelling, too overpowering. His lovemaking demonstrated obvious expertise, and Audra knew it would be very easy to get carried away by it. And she was afraid that after her unguarded disclosure in the vulnerability of the moment that afternoon, Grant might view her as an easy mark. And he wouldn't be too far off, she mocked herself, knowing how she felt about him. One more reason to be careful, since Grant seemed to be able to arouse in her an intensity of feeling that no one since Jimmy ever had. With Jimmy the feelings had been less developed. Of course she was older now, so she supposed her hormones had also matured, she thought wryly.

Telling herself once more to be careful and wondering just how useful her pep talk was going to be this time, Audra reluctantly left the relative security of her tent. Grant was by the fire, feeding it small logs he transferred from the pile under the tree that canopied her tent. Audra was able to study him a moment in the light given off by the riotously jumping flames.

The black jeans and pullover, rather than diminishing his masculine power, gave the impression of unleashing it in the dark of night. His muscles flexed in the smooth, coordinated movements of a dancer, and the light extracted burnished glints from the ebony hair. The straight nose, firm mouth, and strong chin looked invincibly solid in the reddish light bathing them, and her tumultuous thoughts churned as he turned, as always, sensing her presence. He looked at her poised as if in flight, her back protectively seeking the concreteness of the canvas in a maelstrom of feeling, and the raw hunger in his face was tempered to a latent sensuality. And Audra knew that her pep talk would not do her a bit of good under this assault of her senses.

The deep sound of his voice broke her from her frozen stance. "I bought some fresh corn at one of the farms on top of the hill and brought burgundy to go with the steaks."

He stared at her in silent amusement, and Audra belatedly realized she was expected to say something. "Oh sure. Sounds fine. I'm so ravenous I could eat a horse."

Grant's eyebrows rose in a black mocking arch at her inane words, and Audra hurriedly moved to the picnic table to put away the hamburgers she'd been about to cook. She was grateful Grant hadn't said what was obviously going through his mind: that her limp body and equally lackluster words were not suggestive of any great hunger. Or at least, she castigated herself mentally, not for any edibles such as corn or steak.

Resolving to stop acting like an infatuated teenager, Audra slammed the cover of the cooler down after replacing the hamburgers and proceeded to peel and hack an army of potatoes.

The meal was delicious, but consumed in companionable silence. Grant had cooked the steaks to medium-rare for him and well-done perfection for Audra, who couldn't stand the thought of rare meat. The potatoes she had fried with a tomato-and-onion sauce turned out good for a change, and Audra had sighed in inaudible relief when Grant had enthusiastically dug into her contribution to the meal and soon after asked for seconds.

Now, while they waited for the corncobs to roast in their husks, the aromatic smell teasing their nostrils, Audra found herself too wonderfully tired and satiated with food and wine to experience any discomfort or self-consciousness. She vaguely wondered why Grant had such an overpowering effect on her, but drowsily determined it had to be her body waking up and sending her irate signals from long neglected nerve endings. Experiencing the beauty of the cool summer night and the pleasure of the company with newly wakened sensitivity, she wondered why she couldn't just go with her feelings and simply enjoy.

Grant was peacefully quiet and seemed comfortably

content. Audra watched him from underneath heavy lids, his long body stretched on the hard ground, legs extended near the crackling fire, his broad shoulders and head propped up on a large log he'd dragged from a nearby camp, recently vacated.

He swiveled his head slowly, his eyes meeting hers, for once, in silent communion. He studied her, and the smile that only quirked the corners of his mouth reached and warmed his dark blue eyes. Pushing back on his heels, he rose and bent forward to test the corn.

"Done," he announced.

Grant peeled the corn for her and left the base of the husk so she wouldn't burn herself. Handing the corn to Audra and noticing her sudden blinking, he added, "And not a moment too soon."

Audra felt guilty at not helping, but the weeks of rushing and nights of reduced sleep had caught up with her and she felt an overwhelming desire to just curl up on her lounging chair and sleep for a few hours. Better yet, lots of hours. About twenty-four sounded just right. Just lifting her arm and attempting to eat the fresh corn was proving a major undertaking.

Grant gripped her firmly by the waist and moved her bottom to one side of the lounger. Then, sitting down next to her, his hard thigh against the softness of her hip, he commanded softly, "Eat."

Audra automatically opened her mouth, but lost in the darkness of his gaze, she found even the simple task of chewing an effort. Even the kernels did not seem to cooperate. Whereas before they had looked soft and tender, they now clung tenaciously to the woody spike and Audra had the hardest time dislodging them. With Grant so near, the male smell of him attacked and awakened her tired nostrils. His eyes, mirroring the darkness of the summer night, seduced her senses without words.

After getting morsels past the growing constriction in her throat one more time, Audra gave up. "I'm not hungry anymore," she told him. It didn't help to notice that his all-seeing eyes were following the convulsive movement of her throat with great interest. "I guess your steak was more than enough. I can't eat another bite," she added, failing to suppress a gigantic yawn.

His gleaming gaze traveled up her neck and chin, before finally stopping at her eyes. Audra felt the lethargy induced by the good food and wine intensify, incorporating this new assault on her senses. She looked helplessly at Grant, all rational thought fleeing her exhausted mind.

Grant stood up and tossed the corncob into the garbage bag a few feet away and said grimly, "I think you've had enough for the day." He bent and picked her up, letting her feet slide to the ground in order to open the outside zipper of the tent, and shouldering his way past into the long, narrow opening, carried her inside and laid her down gently on the sleeping bag.

It was pitch black inside save for the thin ray of light entering through the small square window which illuminated a corner of the sleeping bag. Grant sat on the edge of the inflated mattress and groped in back of Audra, searching for something. When he found it, he pulled a sleepy Audra upright. "Let's get you into this," he said, and stood up again to leave the tent. Bending his head to clear the side, he opened the flap and threw over his shoulder, "I'll wait outside till you're done."

Audra undressed slowly, savoring the knowledge of

his proximity. And the temptation. Taking her slacks off, she put her pajama bottoms on to counteract the chill that was always a welcome part of camping after the draining heat of the day.

Shivers danced through her as she slipped her wool shirt off and took off her bra. She'd just put on her soft flannel pajama top when Grant came in to check on her.

"Ready?" he asked, resuming his seat next to her on the mattress.

Audra's fingers stopped moving of their own volition, and she murmured haltingly, "Not quite."

Although her blouse gaped open, Audra felt warmth slowly seeping into her at Grant's nearness, his body heat acting more effectively than a thermal blanket. Audra sensed rather than saw when he raised his hand to touch her neck and then moved upward to the top of her head, where he removed her headband and wound his fingers in the silky tresses. His hand played for a delicate, tender moment with her hair and then descended slowly to her throat. Finding that her top was still open, he felt for the buttons and deftly began to close them. The brush of his fingers on her sensitized skin ignited a small flame deep in the center of her body, and Audra could not contain the tiny gasp that escaped her lips.

Grant froze, and only then did Audra realize that his breathing was slightly uneven also. She'd been so enmeshed in her own sensations that she'd failed to notice Grant was affected by her nearness just as strongly.

Audra touched his face shyly, her fingers trembling against the rough masculine cheek. Grant pressed them to his mouth, raining tiny kisses on them. He took her other hand in his, and they remained motionless for a timeless moment, only the seductive rustle of leaves brushing against each other in the slight breeze and the occasional sound of a nocturnal animal interrupting the night stillness. The sexual tension was almost tangible, and Audra felt her stomach muscles contracting.

Grant leaned forward slowly, placing Audra's hands under his sweater, and Audra moaned as her hands came in contact with the moist, firm flesh. She rubbed her palms sensuously over his chest, taking delight in the tickling sensation the rough hairs produced and in the harsh release of breath the action evoked from Grant. He cupped her face in his hands, drawing the outline of her forehead and chin as if wanting to learn her in the dark.

Then his hands were moving lower, and his mouth followed the path his hands had made. He kissed her lips, chin, neck, and when he'd undone the buttons he had begun closing, buried his face in the deep valley between her breasts. Audra could feel her nipples hardening from cold and desire, and as if sensing their pull, his head moved inexorably to one breast, his lips brushing the enlarged crest while a hand stroked her other breast.

The dreamy contentment of the embrace acquired an urgent quality as Grant's hand moved to the waistband of her pajama bottoms and pushed the elastic material down. Grant cupped a hipbone in his hand and then, sliding beneath the lace panties, moved around to make unhurried, sensuous forays over her waist and stomach, turning the fire in its pit into a full blaze as his other hand teased the diamond-hard peak of her breast.

Audra made tiny pleasure sounds deep in her throat, and Grant abandoned possession of her breast to capture and savor them in his mouth. Her throbbing pulse resonated in her ears as the flames Grant was fanning made Audra melt against the hard length covering her. Her hands kneading the smooth muscularity of his back with abandon, Audra arched her body toward his, needing to be closer, ever closer to him.

With an abrupt movement, Grant pulled himself away from her. Audra could not comprehend the withdrawal at first, sensing only an emptiness, a coldness about her body. She tried to wind her arms around his neck and force him near again, find warmth again. But Grant gently disentangled her arms and held them firmly. His voice, when he spoke, was not entirely steady.

"I'd better go, Audra. You're too tired to think clearly now, and I don't want to see hate or regret in those clear green eyes in the morning."

"Not hate, Grant. Not that," denied Audra in an aching voice.

"But regret?"

Audra hoped she'd never regret anything that happened between her and Grant, but she didn't answer, and Grant quickly found the edges of the pajama top and pulled them together, not bothering to close them. Unzipping the sleeping bag with equal rapidity—as if it were of the utmost importance to leave her without delay—he picked her up and laid her carefully inside.

As he zipped the bag back up, Audra, with a brazenness she did not know she possessed, said, "Will you kiss me good night?"

She could sense Grant's hesitation and thought for a moment that he was going to ignore her request. Audra felt his inner struggle and knew a reckless, wild desire for him to take her right then and there. After all, he'd made *his* desire for her quite evident that first day—was it only yesterday?—in the library. And he'd followed her to Devil's Lake and tracked her down in the camping grounds.

But when Grant leaned over, Audra knew he had himself under a tight rein. He obligingly pecked her on the cheek, but she turned her head swiftly so her lips encountered his and the kiss deepened. Audra was aware of the restraint Grant was placing on himself, and one part of her mind that had nothing to do with the delicious havoc she was experiencing as Grant once again probed and drank from the sensual hollows of her mouth was horrified at her teasing. But the other part, the part that seemed to always be on the verge of conquering when Grant was around and certainly was governing her tonight, gloried in the feminine power she had over Grant.

Grant pushed himself away with rigid effort and swore under his breath. When he spoke, his voice was harsh.

"You're lucky tonight, Audra. Real lucky. I'd like to..." He cut himself off, but Audra was not overly concerned with what Grant had been about to say. The warm coziness of the sleeping bag acted with lulling effectiveness, and Grant's very real presence, combating the loneliness and countless empty nights, eased her body into a state of complete relaxation. The last things she noticed before she fell into a deep sleep were the rueful smile on Grant's face as he bent down to place her flashlight within easy reach, the single ray of moonlight touching the rugged planes of his face briefly before he quietly closed the small window, and the butterfly-soft kiss he dropped on her forehead.

- 5 -

AUDRA EMERGED FROM her warm cocoon gradually. Her sleep-befogged mind first registered the sound of hearty voices from surrounding camps and the loud thumps of wood being dumped from the truck making the rounds up the hill to supply campers. Then her reluctant eyelids opened to the subdued light in the tent. She remembered Grant had snapped closed the small window on the right side of the tent and smiled warmly as she stretched luxuriously and encountered the flashlight Grant had put within reach in case she had to get up during the night.

Grant! Her mind came awake with a jolt as last night's events flooded her mind in greater, vivid detail. She sat up suddenly, only to be bounced back by the restraining sleeping bag. She unzipped it with annoyed restlessness and knelt on the soft, warm material. Audra felt a burning heat in every inch of her body and she wondered how she would ever be able to face Grant again.

She pushed back the sleeve of her pajama top and saw it was past eleven. She had slept twelve hours! She must have really been dead on her feet. The combination of hard work lately plus the fresh air and unaccustomed physical exertion had really taken its toll on her, she told herself. But she knew that excuse could not exonerate her behavior with Grant. How in the world could she explain to him? Remembering her uncharacteristic behavior with unfortunately perfect recall, Audra marveled at Grant's control. She had thrown herself at him, and he had correctly guessed she would hate herself in the morning if he'd made love to her, when the needs of her body were not paramount and could be put in the proper perspective. In fact, last night Grant had seemed to know her better than she knew herself. Or had he perhaps not been as involved?

That line of reasoning did not seem too palatable, and Audra decided to shelve it for a while. There was time enough to delve into his motivations and emotions, she told herself. First she had to put her own house in order.

A fresh wave of heat prickled her body as Audra relived Grant's skilled and tender lovemaking, and she nearly groaned aloud at the intense longing that made her nipples stand erect and her body languorous all over again.

Jumping to her feet, she grabbed a robe and towel out of her suitcase, as well as her toiletry bag. She needed a long cold shower.

Since it was already so late, Audra decided against the walk to the shower facilities and took the car. Standing under the stinging cold needles of the shower for almost half an hour did not provide her with any defense before Grant's return. And she knew Grant would be back.

With a sinking feeling, Audra thought that maybe Grant had reconsidered in the light of day and felt she owed him something. She certainly had not made it any easier for him. But something in Audra rebelled at the notion of Grant collecting on a rain check. He hadn't taken advantage of her the night before, when she'd been his for the taking. He would surely be reasonable when she explained to him.

Somewhat reassured, Audra drove back slowly to her campsite, disinclined to return to what she viewed as the scene of her crime. While dressing in forest green slacks and a lime green sleeveless blouse, Audra told herself that the best approach would be to tell Grant the truth. That she had not made love to a man since Jimmy, and that she was not a tease. Not normally, anyway. Ever since she'd met Grant, she had felt an overwhelming need to explain some of her most unwise actions to him, but she had never allowed herself to analyze the reason behind it.

She only knew she was very attracted to Grant, but the suddenness and intensity of the attraction had thrown her off keel. Ever since he'd disarmed her right after she'd put up her tent, Audra was finding it harder and harder to keep from falling into the vortex of his virile magnetism. She had loved Jimmy very much, but there was a night and day difference in her feelings for her husband and those she now felt toward Grant.

The most maddening part of the situation was that she could still taste the pain she'd felt when Jimmy had died. There had been a sense of betrayal, a sense of desolation so profound she'd gone around like a zombie for days. Audra realized with sudden insight that if she'd ever let herself care too deeply for Grant and were to lose him, the pain and sorrow would be even more intense than that she'd experienced over Jimmy's loss.

But the other half of the dilemma was that conducting casual love affairs was not part of her makeup, either. Her body was making demands her mind could no longer ignore, and she wished in sudden desperation that Grant had never come into that library two days ago.

Shaking her head in self-disgust, Audra went to sit disconsolately on the large log Grant had occupied the night before. Her mind had been going in circles so much lately that her head was spinning painfully.

But when Grant turned into her lot and parked his car next to hers and she saw the tall figure emerging from the car with such animal grace and power, all her rationalizations fled and she couldn't hide the eagerness she knew her eyes betrayed.

Grant was the only reality she wanted to deal with right now. She saw the blue-green eyes run quickly over her from the top of her head to the tip of her beige loafers with that gleam she had come to recognize as possessiveness. But something else was present in his glance. Anger? Amusement?

Grant went down on his haunches, and Audra noticed that indeed it was amusement she saw dancing in his eyes. But at what? Audra looked down her front, thinking that perhaps she'd left some buttons undone. But her high-necked pullover blouse did not have any. Her puzzlement was evident in the inquiring glance she gave Grant, and her embarrassment and guilt were put aside for a moment. But they soon returned when he spoke.

"You didn't have to go overboard, Audra. Those tailored slacks and loose blouse might be good and well for a church social, but let me assure you right now that I have not turned into a ravenous beast after last night's episode."

Audra wished she were anywhere but here facing the man who was looking at her with eyes that made her bones melt, but whose mocking smile could at the same time make her so mad and humiliated that she wanted a deep hole to sink into. Preferably one as deep as Jules Verne's center of the earth.

Knowing it would be best if she got it over with, Audra got up, suddenly needing movement. Collecting her thoughts and taking a deep breath, she turned to face Grant.

"Grant, I'm sorry about last night. It seems that since I've met you, all I do is behave stupidly and out of character..."

"Are you sorry because you didn't enjoy it?" Grant cut in smoothly.

"No, of course not!" Audra answered quickly, and bit her tongue at the quickly veiled look of triumph that showed fleetingly in Grant's eyes.

Grant regarded her for a moment silently, and she bravely met his gaze without faltering.

"Then I think you've nothing to feel sorry about. And stop looking so scared. It's I who should apologize for letting things get so out of hand when you were scarcely awake or aware of what you were doing."

Audra stared at him in amazement. She certainly had been aware of what had taken place, and it was that and the fact that she had been the instigator that chewed at her insides. She opened her mouth to speak, but Grant anticipated her.

"Let's talk about this later, after we've gotten some food in you. Are you very hungry?"

Audra shook her head.

"Have you had breakfast?" he asked again, and Audra smiled inwardly at his determination. He really had a one-track mind, and now that she had resolved to do her penance, he wouldn't allow her to do so on an empty stomach.

"No, as I only got up half an hour ago. But—" she tried again.

"I thought as much," he cut in. "You really needed the rest, and that's why I didn't come and get you sooner." Audra wondered if Grant realized how much he over-whelmed her. The way he took command was maddening sometimes, though last night had definitely been mad-dening and frustrating for a different reason. She shook off her daydreams to hear him give another directive. "Then we'll have lunch, and you can show me some of the sights."

Being with Grant was like being on a roller coaster! Audra blinked rapidly, then shrugged her shoulders. There was no fighting this man. "Are we taking my car?" she asked.

Grant frowned and Audra grinned at having thrown him off stride, even if for just an instant. "No. Why?"

"Well, if I'm to show you the sights, don't you think I should be driving? After all, that is the time-honored tradition. The native or connoisseur showing the novice around," she said sweetly.

Grant's lips curved into a smile, laugh lines very much

in evidence in the lean, tanned cheeks. "What are you now, Audra? Twenty-three? Twenty-four?"

Not knowing what that had to do with anything, Audra answered huffily. "Almost twenty-six."

"And I'm almost thirty-five," he mocked. "That gives me almost a decade of living on you, so I doubt the term 'novice' applies to me. And as for 'connoisseur,'" he grinned while she squirmed inwardly, "I think that in a contest I'd win hands down. Not that I'd mind helping you join the ranks," he added, a wicked glint in his eyes.

Audra dug her nails into her sweaty palms and counted to ten. He was the most exasperating, infuriating man! She would never be in his league when it came to sexual innuendos, so she wasn't about to try and do battle.

She stalked to his car and got in without waiting for Grant, who joined her shortly, dwarfing the large, comfortable interior. Audra was just waiting for one more crack, even a chuckle. But Grant drove expertly and quietly, the trip up the steep slope seeming a lot safer and quicker with his self-assured hands on the wheel.

Once on the narrow road leading into Baraboo, he glanced at her and his eyes were filled with merriment. "Calmed down yet?"

Audra realized that yes, she had indeed. She marveled again at his sixth sense in reading her moods and perversely tried to appear still peeved. But another glance of those laughing eyes and a flash of white teeth and she was lost. The smile that had been teasing at the corners of her mouth won out, and Audra gave up trying to contort her face into a disagreeable mask.

"Where would you like to eat?" Grant asked, his eyes tacitly approving her change of mood.

Audra didn't have to think. "Would you mind stopping

at a fast food restaurant? I seem to have slept away a large portion of my vacation, and I'd like to catch up. Unless you're very hungry?"

His eyes were saying, yes, but not for food, and Audra's pulse began racing. But his answer was mild enough. "I had a good breakfast, to answer one part of your question. As for the other, you needed the sleep. A vacation should be used for restoring one's energy, not dissipating it. You can think of those extra hours you slept as a charging of batteries."

Audra laughed and she noticed Grant gaze at her mouth. She moistened her lips automatically, then immediately pulled her tongue back inside her dry mouth as she noticed the smoldering glitter in Grant's eyes.

His raw virility made her ill at ease again, and she reconsidered whether coming out with Grant had been such a good idea after all. But she knew that were she back in Devil's Lake, she'd be waiting anxiously for him, longing for him, and torturing herself with memories of last night. Audra sighed, thinking that she was damned if she did, damned if she didn't.

Her sigh had apparently been audible, because Grant took her hand in his and gave it a reassuring squeeze. Then he placed her hand on his thigh, and putting his arm around her shoulders, pulled her across the seat to sit close to him. Audra's hand on his thigh tightened convulsively, and she forced herself to relax it. She let her fingers rest lightly on the hard column of flesh and after a while was able to relax her whole body, liking the warmth and scent of Grant's body next to hers and the feel of muscles in his right leg flexing with each movement.

*   *   *

Waiting in line with Grant, Audra thought she'd never felt more alive in ages. Lunch had been a quick, pleasant affair because Audra was impatient to go on the amphibious Ducks and Grant had kept all talk neutral.

Grant had left the day's activities to her choosing, and Audra had elected to go on to the combination land-water ride, since much of the day was already over.

One of the remodeled boats, remnants of World War II and repainted in cheerful colors, came back from a previous ride. Children started jumping in gleeful anticipation, and parents had to keep them from rushing into the stairs, sternly reprimanding the excited children to wait their turn.

As they were going up the dark green steps to climb into the double-purpose vehicle, Audra stumbled and reached for the white railing. She would have fallen flat on her face but for Grant's arm, which shot out and dug into her slender waist, preventing a very ignominious tumble. He kept his arm around her until she was settled in her seat.

Audra leaned back comfortably, warmly aware of Grant's arm draped on the seat in back of her. She looked happily at the green-and-white striped canvas roof of their Duck and breathed the pine-scented air. The day was perfect, with not a cloud marring the smoothness of the radiant sky.

"You're looking very pleased with yourself," Grant told her softly, smiling.

Audra smiled back. "I am. I haven't been here since . . ." she wrinkled her nose while she thought about it and then said with some surprise, ". . . since the summer after I graduated high school. I was a tour guide here, and as much as I loved the place from all those yearly camping trips with my parents, I found I ended up liking it even more as I learned more of the history of the region."

"Do you remember anything from your lectures?" Grant asked.

Audra gave him a long look to see if he was pretending an interest out of politeness.

Reading her mind, Grant smiled and said, "I really am interested."

"Okay, then. Let's see . . . oh, yes." She turned in her seat, brushing a lock of hair away from her eyes. "For example, the Indian legends said a great snake created the dells with the slithering motion of its body. But I was forced to tell visitors—for the sake of fairness, you understand—" Audra grinned impishly, "that geologists had a more prosaic explanation. They claim that the dells were created fifteen thousand years ago by the runoff waters of receding glaciers. The torrent of water carved through the sandstone, leaving behind a seven-mile stretch containing nature's sculptures, such as Stand Rock, Witch's Gulch, Cold Water Canyon, Fat Man's Misery, and Devil's Elbow."

"Leave it to a geologist to intrude with such sobering practicality," Grant murmured.

Audra, who had averted her face for a moment to look at the verdant profusion on her side of the road, turned her head swiftly at something in his tone and asked suspiciously, "What *do* you do, anyway?"

"I'm a geologist."

The laughter that bubbled to her lips could not be suppressed and Audra didn't try, either. Grant's deep chuckle joined her laughter, and even though she noticed the amused glances of fellow tourists, Audra could not stop for a long while.

Their guide, who had built up their ride for all it was worth in benefit of the round-eyed, eager children, asked for absolute silence as they completed their drive through the Duck trails. As instructed by Bill, their college-age guide, everyone held his breath for the plunge into the green waters. He made a dramatic production of it, telling them it was good practice for his theater-arts degree, and adults could be heard joining the laughter, squeals, and screams of the children as the amphibious vehicle left land for water with a resounding splash.

The rest of the ride was more peaceful, and the children were able to tone down their enthusiasm to a low roar. Their guide traded jokes back and forth with the visitors, as well as information on the dells' river and formations, and all too soon they were back at the starting point.

Before returning to the car, Audra and Grant took a leisurely walk, his arm circling her shoulders, her arm looping around the narrow masculine waist. The smell of wild flowers was in the air, and it intermingled in fragrant confusion with the lemon-lime aftershave that still lingered on Grant's tanned face. A strong breeze whipped Audra's hair against her mouth, and a sun-streaked strand stuck persistently between her lips. Grant twisted her around, and picking up the golden-brown lock that hit against her cheek and mouth time and time again, rubbed the silky hair for a second before curling it behind her ear.

By silent mutual consent, they walked toward the car, their arms about each other, Audra marveling at the perfect fit of their bodies.

- *6* -

ONCE THEY WERE back in the car, Grant turned in his seat to face Audra. "We have to talk, Audra, but I think we need more time and certainly more quiet and seclusion than we had back there."

"I'm sorry, Grant. I didn't think that you might be bored by the ride."

"I wasn't. It's been a long time since I enjoyed myself so much. But we have to talk about last night, and I'd like to do so uninterrupted." Audra nodded her agreement, knowing her reprieve from explaining about last night wouldn't last forever.

Grant shifted to start the car. "What time shall I pick you up for dinner?" he asked as they entered the traffic on the main road.

Audra thought quickly. She wanted to take her time showering and dressing. "Seven-thirty?"

Grant inclined his head in assent. "Any place special?"

"Surprise me," she told him. Then, remembering their phone conversation of two nights ago, she accused softly, "You still haven't apologized for not telling me that you knew I was coming here."

Grant laughed. "What about you and that visit to your parents, who you hadn't seen in such a long time?"

"Well, what did you expect," Audra said defensively. "I didn't know you..." And I still don't, she added silently, despite what her body and senses told her.

"Exactly," Grant grinned. "And now you'll get a chance to. Tonight you can ask whatever questions are hovering in that pretty head of yours."

The rest of the trip was conducted in silence, except for occasional comments on the scenery. Audra stole glances at his chiseled profile and saw his wide forehead furrowed in thought several times. She enjoyed the quiet companionship after the crowded, noisy fun of the ride, and leaning back on the reclining seat, let the fingers of the breeze cool her warm cheeks and slide through her hair, wondering what revelations that evening would bring.

Audra felt a delightful sense of anticipation curl her insides as she slipped on her violet dirndl dress. She had only had a few casual dates since Jimmy's death, but even these had ceased during the past few months. Audra was determined to finish her degree and join the working force and had sacrificed her social life to do it. Until now, though, she reflected, it had not seemed much of a sacrifice since none of the men she'd met had really interested her. Everyone she'd dated now seemed a pale imitation of Grant. Even Jimmy's image and the painful memories had receded with the force of Grant's vitally male presence.

She smiled at the incongruity of dressing up for dinner in her tent. She had not told Grant that the reason she had wanted extra time was to pick up a dress. She had only brought shorts, slacks, and a couple of skirts with her, anticipating only sportslike activities. But she wanted to look special tonight and was glad to have found this simple dress in one of Baraboo's stores.

Audra had planned on wearing her hair in a sophisticated chignon, but negotiating the pins with one hand while holding up her mirror with the other proved impossible. Since Grant would be arriving any minute now, she didn't want to miss him by running down to the ladies' bathroom at the base of the hill. Finally, with an unladylike epithet, she let her hair fall in a soft mass and threaded a violet velvet ribbon through its gleaming thickness.

She added a matching ribbon around her neck, glad she'd thought of picking up an extra length, and was pleased at the way its darkness provided a touch of evening elegance and contrasted nicely with the lilac lacing on the square-cut neckline and cap sleeves.

Her piecemeal reflection in the small mirror told her that if not sophisticated, she at least looked freshly attractive for her dinner date with Grant.

She heard the soft hum of his car as she was picking up her white clutch purse from the sleeping bag and hastily readjusted the strap on her white high-heeled sandal. Snuffing out the lantern, Audra pushed aside the tent's flap.

Grant was putting out her campfire, and her breath

caught in her throat at his appearance. His gray slacks emphasized the muscular length of his legs, and the navy blazer fitted the breadth of his shoulders with tailored precision.

Audra began walking forward slowly, and Grant's eyes gleamed as she was bathed for a moment in the last blaze from the fire. Then he straightened, draped a casual arm around her shoulders and, lifting her chin, dropped a soft kiss on her parted lips.

"You smell delicious," he complimented as he guided her carefully over the rough gravel to the car a few yards away.

"So do you," countered Audra, inhaling the fresh masculine scent of him mingled with lemon-lime aftershave.

"Now do you believe me when I tell you we're perfectly compatible?" He laughed with that deep sound that brought goose pumps to skin already sensitized by his presence.

Audra chose to ignore his comment and got into the car quickly. Grant always managed to throw her off balance, and she thought it unfair of him to make constant references to their first encounter, which she'd just as soon forget, and she told him as much.

"Forget it? Why?" Grant sounded genuinely puzzled.

"Why?" Audra retorted. "Because I don't conduct myself with such abandon at the drop of a hat, that's why," she told him, her voice thick with mortification. "And it is awfully embarrassing for me to remember our first meeting..."

Grant picked up the hand that had been fidgeting nervously with the purse in her lap and rubbed circles on the inside of her palm with his thumb. "Nothing that happens between us should ever embarrass you, Audra," he said gently.

Audra felt a lump rise in her throat and blinked back the sudden wetness in her eyes. She couldn't think of anything to say, so she just let her hand remain in his firm grasp and fought the waves of weakness his caressing motion induced.

Grant drove slowly down the road which led to the main trailer section of the park. There were a couple of camping parties in motion, complete with guitar singing and marshmallow roasting over the hearty fires. The sounds receded gradually as they moved out of the park, and the night settled into a tranquil silence broken only by the occasional swishing of a car until they got to Wisconsin Dells.

Driving through downtown Wisconsin Dells was an experience in itself. Eye-catching posters depicted all the attractions offered: Stand Rock Ceremonial, Fort Dells, Haunted Mansion. Traveling through it at night did not detract from its vibrant charm but rather added a new facet to it.

The historic River Inn came into view, and Audra admired the elegance of the resort overlooking the upper dells. Grant let go of her hand shortly and maneuvered the car into a parking spot, then came around to open the door for her.

It took a few seconds for Audra to get used to the soft light inside after the stygian darkness, and then Grant was leading her to a seat by the window with a magnificent view of the dark water and the myriad lights spotting its glassy surface.

The waiter approached them almost immediately, and

they ordered cocktails—Scotch on the rocks for Grant and a Pink Lady for Audra.

Grant leaned back negligently in his tall-backed chair, and Audra, aware of his searching glance, broke the disconcerting silence.

"You mentioned you were a geologist?" she asked leadingly, hoping that talking about his job would at least give her a glimmer of the man behind the agile mind and superb body.

"It's what I originally set out to do," Grant answered obligingly, his eyes clearly revealing his amusement. "Only at the age of twenty, with one year of college left, I had to drop out of school and help with my father's business. For two years I breathed and lived financial statements and balance sheets day and night. It had turned out my father's trusted partners had embezzled quite a bit of the firm's funds."

"Couldn't your mother help?" Audra asked, thinking that it had been a big responsibility to level at a twenty-year-old.

"My mother had died the previous year from cancer, after a three-year battle. My father had neglected the business to be at her side, and between my mother's death and the pillaging of his brain child by people he had considered his family, he had a heart attack. I instituted safeguards to prevent anything similar from happening again, but he never recovered from my mother's death or his disillusionment. He died of a massive coronary five years ago."

Audra looked at him mutely, not knowing what words to use. Saying "I'm sorry" seemed so inadequate. Although his voice had been even and his eyes expressionless, she felt pain for him and he covered her hand with his own with a reassuring smile.

"But you still persisted about being a geologist?"

Grant nodded and picked up his drink. "After the company was back on its feet, my father took over part-time. After his death, I became chairman of the board, but my main interest is still geology. I went back to school full-time and worked for an advanced degree. The company is a minor interest."

"You must travel a great deal," Audra said with unconscious yearning, thinking of all the places he must have visited and which she had only dreamed of—Africa, Arabia, India, Egypt.

"Some," he answered briefly. "But tell me about yourself," he changed the direction of the conversation smoothly. "What have you been so diligently researching?"

"Urban anthropology," she answered, taking a sip of her own drink. The ice cream had now dissolved to a more malleable consistency, and Audra automatically licked her upper lip free of the creamy substance, until she noticed his interested glance.

"I had a bachelor of science in anthropology, but my master's combines both anthropology and sociology. I've always been interested in the science of man, and I think that studying other cultures and the history of mankind prepares us to find solutions to today's problems. The Indian concept of land is a perfect example. The pioneers and Indians could not subsist peacefully side by side because the Indian saw land as communal property." Audra leaned forward in her chair, becoming enthusiastic as she warmed to her subject. "And property is not even the right word for it because they do not envision that anyone can actually own the land. And in view of the desperate and last-minute measures now put forth by conservationists and ecologists, history is teaching us who had the right view of land: the sacred world view of the Indian or the consumerism of the whites." Suddenly aware she had been rambling, as always when she became caught up with her favorite theme, Audra bit her lip. "I'm sorry if I've been boring you..."

"Not at all," Grant denied with obvious sincerity. "It's just surprising to see anyone feel that strongly about things anymore."

Their waiter approached them to ask if they wanted another drink, but both Grant and Audra declined, choosing instead to order.

"When did you find time to marry?" Grant asked her when the waiter moved away.

It was the question she'd been dreading, but there was no avoiding it. Without looking at Grant, tracing circles on the snowy linen with a gleaming fork, Audra answered softly. "I met my husband my sophomore year. He was a senior and president of a fraternity. We met at a Greek party one of my friends had talked me into attending, telling me I spent too much time studying."

"Audra, look at me." Grant commanded gently.

Audra raised her head and found Grant regarding her with a tenderness she found breathtaking. She stopped playing with the fork, and laying it on the table, continued steadily, "I really disliked that particular fraternity, and when I first saw Jimmy, I thought he was like all the rest of the boys. He was with a date, a beautiful blonde who had been elected Greek queen the previous semester."

"But Jimmy had eyes only for you," Grant interjected teasingly.

"I wouldn't go that far," Audra said in a lighter tone. "He still had that girl clinging adhesively to his arm." Audra heard the slight note of jealousy in her voice even after all these years, but could not help it. She had never liked to share. She saw by the dancing lights in Grant's eyes that he had noticed, but he didn't comment. "He didn't get rid of the girl or anything. Jimmy was too good and decent for anything like that." Her voice broke as she thought of the inherent kindness present in all of Jimmy's actions. "But he did ask me for my phone number. And a year later we were married."

"What did your parents have to say about that?"

"The expected. But I was too busy living in my perfect little world to worry much about their feelings or reactions," Audra said with self-directed bitterness. "I was prepared to stay at home, even drop out of school if necessary. But Jimmy encouraged me to pursue my studies, saying that I was too young to have children and that he wanted me to himself for a while."

"Did you resent him for that?"

Audra sighed, knowing that at one point in the grief-stricken weeks following his death she had even blamed him for that.

"Not anymore. In retrospect, I see he was right about a lot of things. Especially when he kept me from abandoning my studies. He'd told me, 'You never know what might happen.'" Her voice cracked again, and she hastily took a sip of water. "When they notified me of the accident, I was really glad to have my parents around."

"I think your parents must have been glad to offer you comfort at the time also," Grant told her gently in response to the self-accusatory note in her voice.

Audra looked at him through a misty veil. "They were.

They tried to get me to come home, but I wanted to stand on my own two feet. I was tired of leaning on someone."

"But you still are."

Audra stared at Grant with incredulity. "I'm living alone, Grant. And I'm supporting myself."

"But you're still leaning on Jimmy. And his memory. You've been hurt badly, and at a young age, so you've kept a wall around yourself to prevent getting hurt again."

"Grant. I'd just turned twenty-one when I was made a widow. My husband has been dead for over three years," Audra insisted, trying to make him understand. "We'd only been married for fourteen months, and you can't expect a person . . ."

"And what have you been doing with yourself for the past few years?" Grant interjected, his tone becoming harsh.

As comprehension dawned on Audra, so did the beginning of anger. "I see. You think I should have greeted the news of my husband's death with a party and mourned him by jumping into bed with any man that happened along," she said icily.

"Don't be childish, Audra," Grant said with weary patience. "You're so afraid of becoming involved again that you've kept yourself on ice since Jimmy's death. In that sense, you have not matured in the past three years. You are at the same emotional age you were when your husband was taken away from you."

Audra conveniently ignored the little voice that was burning into her brain, acknowledging the truth of some of his statements. Her only thought was to strike back at the man who had accurately pinpointed her life for the past three years, making her take a good look at herself.

"I can't believe what I'm hearing," Audra hissed.

"And I thought that I had to apologize to you about last night. But I see that I should be thankful things didn't go any farther. You're just one more of those men who think that a divorced or widowed woman is fair game."

Her hand struck blindly at her side for her clutch purse, and she began to rise.

"Sit down, Audra." Grant's expression was unchanged, but there was a hardening in the blue-green gaze that effectively halted her. With slow, deliberate movements, she sank back down on her seat and put her purse on the chair by her side. "If what you accuse me of is true, then why didn't I take what you so freely offered last night?" he asked quietly.

Audra felt the heat of remembered shame steal up into her cheeks and said nastily, "Perhaps you were afraid I'd fall asleep in the middle of the act."

She didn't think his eyes could become any flintier, but they did. She saw with relief the trolley approach their table, laden with food, and smiled at the waiter who uncovered steaming, aromatic dishes.

Audra knew her reprieve was only temporary, and the meal was consumed in total silence. She was only able to pick at her delicious lobster, but Grant finished his steak with no apparent problem. When he asked her if she would like any dessert, Audra shook her head and Grant signaled for their check.

Once outside, he guided her to the car with the flat of his large hand against her waist, his warmth transmitted to her flesh through the flimsy material of her dress. He didn't open the door for her right away but leaned a hip against the car.

"I think you've realized by now that your remark was not only off base but totally unfair," he said slowly.

Audra had regretted it as soon as it had left her lips, but would not admit it in a million years. She thought she had managed her life admirably so far and did not particularly enjoy being called an adolescent by Grant. When she shivered from the night breeze, which carried a cool, light mist from the river, Grant took off his jacket and draped it around her shoulders, keeping it in place with his hands. Audra could feel the warmth of his knuckles against the flesh above the square-cut neckline and trembled again. She stared up into his eyes, absently registering the paleness of his light blue turtleneck shirt against the dark tan of his face and throat.

"I wouldn't normally take such an enlightened view of a woman leading me on as you did last night," Grant said, ignoring the stiffening of Audra's body under his hands, "but I realize you're still trying to come to grips with your emotions. I do think someone needs to make you come alive again. But I won't be made to fit into the mold of your teenage lover, nor will I force you to respond and come to terms with your own needs. You were looking for seduction last night," he continued, and at Audra's gasp grabbed her shoulders as though to shake some sense into her, "but I won't be pushed into a role of seducer. I want a woman who knows her own mind and can admit and recognize her own instincts and desires for what they are—natural."

Audra literally saw red. The gall of the man! She grabbed his wrists to push his hands away from her, but Grant waved them away as if they were flies. "Calm down!" he told her roughly.

"Let go of me!" Audra cried, trying to twist her upper body away from his steel grip.

Grant finally complied, just when she thought her

struggles would leave her a limp rag at his feet.

The drive back to camp was accomplished a lot faster than the one into town, and Audra hugged the corner of the spacious interior, warily eyeing Grant from time to time. He seemed ready to pounce.

Audra got out without assistance as soon as he pulled into her lot, and walked to her tent with a mumbled, "Good night." *Thank you for the evening* would have gotten stuck in her throat.

But Grant caught up with her quickly and twisted her around with an ungentle grip of her upper arm, forcing her chin up with his other hand before she could pull away. She read fury and contempt in his eyes before his face blocked out the moonlight and he kissed her with a savage ruthlessness that precluded any response on her part.

Lifting his head abruptly, he breathed two words in her ear, "Grow up," before he pushed her away from him and got into his car, disappearing into the night while she sought the support of a tree to keep from falling.

- 7 -

TWO HOURS LATER, after an endless, restless turning on the confining narrowness of her uncovered sleeping bag from which she had rolled onto the hard canvas-covered ground several times, Audra disgustedly got up. Even though the night was cool, she felt horribly warm and took her pajama bottoms off, hoping to ease her discomfort.

But after pacing up and down her tent for twenty minutes, during which her usually mild vocabulary became steamier with each stubbing of her toes against her luggage and assorted belongings and constant tripping over her sleeping bag, Audra decided she'd had enough.

Grant's whispered words reverberated in her mind like echoes from the Grand Canyon as she snatched off her top in sudden decision. How dare he accuse her of being childish! She was a woman, not some whimpering virgin of seventeen—or nineteen, as had been her case. Just because she'd sworn off physical and emotional intimacy for almost four years did not make her a coward—it merely made her not the promiscuous type.

As Audra searched for a blouse and slacks, perspiration covered her body in a fine film, fury rising her body temperature to an intolerable degree. Wasn't he the one who had held back the evening before, she asked herself righteously as she jammed on her jeans and blouse. Didn't she have the right to be hesitant? After all, she hadn't had a lover in four years. So where did he get off passing judgment on her?

Stalking out of her tent, Audra contained her temper until she left the camping grounds. Most campers kept regular hours—early to bed and early to rise—and she didn't want to disturb the sleepy peace of the camp with a revving of the motor. Once on the highway, though, Audra let her foot grind into the accelerator. The road was deserted and it suited her mood just fine.

The drive to Grant's motel was one of the fastest in her life, and while one part of her mind was thanking her lucky stars no policeman was witness to her suicide course, another part was preparing a list of the things she was going to say to Grant.

Resisting the urge to screech to a halt in front of his room, Audra closed the car door quietly and sprinted to his room. About to knock on the door, Audra was hit with the thought that he might very well be entertaining someone at this hour of the night. Her uncertainty swiftly changed. Grant was a fast worker when it came to the opposite sex, but he couldn't be *that* fast!

Grant answered her urgent knocks after what seemed an inordinate amount of time, his expression sleepy, his obviously naked body covered by a short terry robe he was still closing as he opened the door.

The obvious concern mirrored in his eyes aroused momentary guilt in Audra, but it was quickly chased away by the realization that while she had been fuming with indignation and awakened desires in the solitude of her tent, Grant had been enjoying the sleep which had proved so elusive to her.

Sweeping into the room, Audra told him sweetly, "I see you've been sleeping the sleep of a clear conscience. Or could it be that you haven't one?"

Grant's worried look turned to one of amusement. He closed and locked the door behind her, and crossing his arms over his wide chest, leaned back against it, his darkened eyes roving coolly over her tense figure.

"Oh I have one, all right." He smiled mockingly. "But I think what's ailing you is of a totally different nature."

"What's ailing me," Audra retorted caustically, "is your unfounded accusations. You passed judgment on me without knowing all the facts, and I resent such sweeping condemnation and closed-mindedness."

"And you couldn't wait till morning to tell me all this?"

Audra's rage grew incandescent, fueled by his calm, amused tone. Her feelings, repressed for years as she strove to forget and bury herself under layers of work and research, surfaced violently. Audra advanced on him with clenched fists, her body painfully taut, wanting to wipe that knowing expression off the handsome face.

He straightened slowly from the door, moving to meet her, and suddenly her precarious control broke. Her hands moved of their own accord, and she began to beat at the broad shoulders, her blows increasing at the quiet laugh vibrating through him and then decreasing as Audra became aware of the warmth and clean scent of his skin.

"That's it, let it all out." Grant didn't attempt to stop her, but put his arms about her, bracing her shaking body with his own until at last she grew calmer and her body absorbed the solidness and warmth of his.

Reason slowly returned, and with it a wave of self-consciousness. Audra did not remember ever having lost control in such a manner, in fact had not cried after Jimmy's death, because his parents had leaned on her after the death of their only child. And the fact that Grant was able to incite her to such heights of emotion frightened her.

As her body relaxed, his hold subtly changed from protectiveness to passion. His hands began to knead the tense muscles of her back, easing her with sure, circular motions. Audra opened the eyes she had closed as her raging hurt had spent itself, and blinked in the sudden soft glare, looking wide-eyed into his face, only inches from hers. His eyes were almost ebony, glittering with desire, and his tan had a darker color beneath it. With inflaming slowness, he lowered his head to light a burning trail of kisses from brow to ear. His tongue stroked the area beneath her ear, where a tiny pulse raced madly, and then entered the rosy shell, exploring its delicate perfection before probing the sensitive skin of her nape and the scented hollow of her neck.

Audra felt the insistent stirring of desire and made an instinctive movement of protest, seeking escape. Her brain was fuzzily telling her she had come to berate Grant, to make him apologize for his unfeeling, unfair treatment of her.

But her body only remembered the abortive passion of another night and overruled her rational capacity, clouding it with the suffocating fumes of desire. His hands roamed her back, then disposed of the buttons on her blouse and slid underneath it to caress her ribcage and waist, before returning once more to her back, moving down from the satiny skin of her shoulders to her hips and below, curving about the twin cheeks of her bottom. His lips rubbed sensuously against hers and then plundered her mouth deeply and persuasively, firing her senses with their demanding claim. Her trembling hands slid the robe open all the way, and the wiry dark hair which curled up the center of his muscular chest tingled her exploring fingers.

He lifted his head for a moment, and his eyes burned into her face. "Tell me," he murmured huskily.

Audra looked at him mutely and tried to fight down the hot waves of longing that were sweeping over her. She knew what he wanted but could not bring herself to say it. Grant waited a moment, searching her flushed face, and when she remained silent, grabbed her wrists gently and pulled her arms away from him. Taking a deep, ragged breath, he told her evenly, "Good night, Audra."

Audra felt herself pale but didn't move toward the door. Instead, she raised trembling hands to the blouse which now gaped open and slowly slipped it off, combating the impulse to cover her braless breasts, hoping to tell him with her actions that which she could not yet formulate into words. Grant muttered a soft curse, and picking up the yellow top she'd let slip through nerveless fingers, thrust it at her and said harshly, "I don't want an easy lay, Audra. I want you, and have told you as much. If you can't own up to the same honest emotion, then you'd better leave."

He tied the belt of his white robe in a rough movement, and his eyes challenged her. Audra hated him for an instant. He was not making things easier for her. Unshed tears stung her eyes and she told him in a low voice, "If you set out to humiliate me, you've succeeded brilliantly." She turned her back on him, intending to button her top, when his arms suddenly circled her waist, drawing her against him.

"Humiliate you? Is it shameful for you to admit that you might want someone as badly as someone wants you?" He turned her around and cupped her chin with his hand. "I know it's not verbalizing your thoughts and feelings that's the trouble, because you have a marvelous, inventive vocabulary at your command. So what is it? Do you really believe I'm out to embarrass you?"

Audra looked into the opalescent depths of his eyes and saw raw, unadulterated desire. The intensity of his emotion, which he made no effort to hide or diminish, freed her. Although it had never been easy for her to express her feelings openly, with Grant there had been an element not present before—fear. Fighting it and trying to banish the shadows from the past, she put her arms around his neck and told him in a clear voice, "I want you. I want you to make love to me."

Grant crushed her into his embrace and a muffled groan shuddered free of his throat as he bent his head to capture her mouth and delicately tease the inside of her lip. Audra quivered with pleasure and returned the caress, as her right hand encircled his neck and her left curled into the silken texture of his thick, raven hair. He drew her even closer to him, one hand low on her hips so that she felt the lean hardness of his body. The muscled length of his thighs made her want to part her legs to accommodate him and she moved against him. Grant's breath quickened as he left her mouth to bury his head in the deep valley between her breasts. Audra's nails curled into the firm masculine back when she felt the tantalizing softness of his lips on her pink peak. She felt the pressure that swelled against her, the pulsating heat of his manhood as it sought closer intimacy. As his mouth covered hers again and swallowed her stifled moan, Grant picked her up and carried her to the bed, where he laid her gently on its cool surface.

Sitting down on the edge, feasting his eyes on her heaving breasts, he reached out and caressed her again so that the white satiny flesh hardened beneath his fingers. Audra stirred and moaned, then blindly lifted her arms to pull his head down so that his lips could follow where his hands had been, holding his head against her as wave after wave of desire ran through her, making her groan and whisper his name over and over again. Then he was lying next to her, his body initiating another sensual shock as skin met skin and she realized he'd taken off his robe. She opened her eyes languidly and murmured, "Please, Grant now... now..." as she felt the unbearable tension inside her screaming to be released.

Grant divested her quickly of her jeans and panties and then caressed her thighs before parting them and sliding between them. At the last moment, her body tensed in a violent stiffening jerk and he held off, supporting his weight with his elbows as his lips and teeth returned to her breasts and nibbled her nipples into a pulsating hardness.

Audra's body relaxed again, and as Grant gently lowered himself above her, she stared into the scorching depths of his eyes. Grant moved into her slowly and then built an easy, even tempo until Audra clung to his back and moaned urgently. She felt him go rigid, checking himself to make sure she was joining him on their fiery journey, and at the last minute, although he had brought her to a peak of pleasure so intense Audra didn't think she could bear it, she found she was holding off, restraining her response.

Audra came back down from the summit reluctantly, securely locked in his arms, but had barely touched ground when his expert caresses began to fan the still warm embers of desire and she heard him warn, "I don't want you halfway, Audra. This time there'll be no holding back."

As the embers burst into flames, Audra felt the heat searing her limbs and she opened them to receive Grant, who fanned the blaze into an all-consuming fire. This time he was not gently controlled but drove her steadily into a land where only the two of them existed, and she was suspended, divorced from any reality but the synchronized movement of their bodies. At the culmination of their passion, Audra soared along with Grant, and the uninhibited sensuality he had unleashed with the escalating torture of her senses left her completely exhausted, so that when the raging fire had receded, Audra was clinging weakly to his moist shoulders.

When he made love to her a third time, Audra did not attempt any evasion or resistance. She welcomed his embrace after the short interlude with a driving need of her own and gave herself to Grant with no physical reservations, the equally devastating climax overwhelming her so that she floated instantly into a deep sleep.

- *8* -

AUDRA WOKE UP by degrees, her body pleasurably relaxed and languorous. Feeling a weight on her stomach, she opened her eyes and looked down, smiling at the brown hand splayed against her white skin. Turning her head, Audra felt a wave of tenderness wash over her at the youthful cast of Grant's features in sleep. His black hair tousled and falling in thick waves over his forehead, his face had a boyish look which was not visible when awake. Then his sheer vitality, intelligence, and maturity created an aura of power and undiluted dynamism which relegated to the background any carefree characteristic.

With intense care, Audra lifted his hand from her body. Chills raced up and down her body as she recalled how that same hand had calmed her initial nervousness and fear and had caressed her into a sweet frenzy. A diffuse blush covered her body at the memory of his

81

refusal to accept a restrained response to his lovemaking. Audra had been afraid to let go, as he'd correctly guessed. And although she had managed to keep a mental reserve, her body had surrendered totally at the onslaught of his unrelenting sensuality.

She managed to get out of bed without disturbing him and padded barefoot on the blue carpet, turning to look at him one more time before entering the bathroom. His body was still in the same position, facing the place her body had occupied; his hand lay on the warm spot she'd vacated. The sight of the lean, bronzed body started a heat within her which quickly spread outward. Her eyes hungrily roamed over wide shoulders, tapering black mat of hair which continued uninterrupted below the inward navel, the narrow hips and flat, corded stomach, the long, powerful legs and shapely calves. Feeling her breathing quicken and her heartbeat accelerate, Audra quickly pivoted and ran into the bathroom, welcoming the cool ceramic as she sat on the edge of the tub and let the water run for her bath.

Audra regretted not having some bubble soap, but reflected she'd not come to stay last night—at least not consciously. She decided to make do with Grant's bar, disdaining the small one provided by the motel, which, besides not lathering to her satisfaction, was a horror to locate against the white bottom when it slipped from one's hand.

Grant's soap had a lemon smell and Audra used it liberally, lathering herself with abandon. In a short time, the bath water was filmy with soap, and after washing her legs, stretching first one, then the other, high in the air with feline satisfaction, she slid further into the tub and let her head rest against the side, intending to relax in the now lukewarm water for a while.

"Don't do that." The husky voice so startled Audra that she slipped and submerged completely with a loud splashing and whaling of arms, the hair she had so carefully pinned up now straggling down her forehead and cheeks as she came up sputtering.

Grant's twitching mouth did not help matters. Besides having had the breath knocked out of her, she had swallowed a few gulpfulls of soapy water and now looked like a drowned rat. Audra felt that Grant's halfhearted attempt to contain his mirth was the absolute limit.

He straightened from his reclining position against the doorjamb and slowly walked toward her. "I don't think it's quite fair for you to hide that delicious body under some opaque water which does not do you full justice," he told her as he reached the side of the bathtub and looked down on her from his imposing height, hands on slim hips.

Audra had been too upset at first to even notice he was naked, but the powerful male thighs on a level with her face jolted her into tingling awareness. Audra felt a shyness which had been erased by Grant's tender, exquisite lovemaking during the night, and she half turned in the rapidly cooling water to let the water out and turn on the shower, intending to rinse the soapy film off her body and get out of the tub in cowardly retreat.

Grant's hand closed over hers, halting her hurried, clumsy movements. He plugged the drainer and turned on the hot water, gripping Audra firmly by the shoulder and forcing her to sit down again. Audra kept her face averted and her body stiffened as she felt both of his hands on her shoulders.

"Remember what I said yesterday, Audra?" She shook

her head, finding it impossible to talk normally when every instinct was telling her to flee. When she wouldn't answer, Grant shifted his body slightly and placed one hand on her chin, forcing her to look at him. "What's the matter sweetheart?"

Her eyes flew to his at the endearment, uttered with such passion and longing. She remembered what he'd said—that she should never feel embarrassed by anything that happened between them. She also recalled that he had promised not to use love words. But after totally possessing her last night, Audra reflected that he couldn't be blamed. She felt uncomfortable about his referring to her as anything but Audra. She still felt afraid—if anything, her fear had increased, and she wanted to keep their intimacy on a physical level. She was walking a tightrope of emotion and was not being very successful at remaining uninvolved—especially when Grant wove his magic spell around her with every look, every touch, and every endearment.

He leaned forward to turn off the hot water, and a hint of a smile appeared on her tremulous lips as she held his gaze unwaveringly and told him softly, "It's just that I was a virgin when I married Jim, and I haven't— well, what I mean is, I haven't been to bed with anyone since, and . . ."

Grant cut through her painful explanation and rubbed his knuckles against her chin. "Do you think I don't know that, kitten? You were insatiable last night—I have the scars to prove it."

Audra's shyness began to ebb and was quickly replaced by indignation. "Me, insatiable? What about you? You acted as if you hadn't had sex in years."

"Oh I've had sex, all right," he drawled, his eyes

gleaming a dark blue in the dim light. "But I have not made love in years."

His statement sobered her. But she was still too mad about her dunking and his all-too-true charge to drop her belligerent attitude and engage in what her body was traitorously demanding.

"I think, Mr. Williams, that you're not much of a gentleman. I've said it before and no doubt will say it again." Warming to her subject, she continued, "Do you know what you are? I'll tell you—"

Her sentence was never finished because he leaned forward, and cupping his hand about her neck, held her head in place while he pillaged her mouth with savage hunger. His tongue moved over the smooth enamel of her teeth, licking one row and then another, and then moved past its barrier into the sweetness within. Audra gasped and the tip of her tongue met his in reciprocal need, but after teasing her for a brief moment, he raised his head, leaving her unsatisfied.

"I don't like the bed when you leave it. It felt quite cold and empty, without this . . . and this . . . and this . . ." he said, moving his hands from her face to her breasts, past her concave stomach to her silken thighs.

"Did I wake you?" Audra asked, her breath coming in short spurts.

"Not intentionally. But I sensed your absence right away," he murmured, reversing his journey across her body with lazy pleasure.

"You seemed so tired, I decided you needed your beauty sleep," Audra teased daringly.

Grant smiled and took a sharp, playful nip of her earlobe. "As I recall, you fairly passed out after the third time we made love."

Audra felt heat steal into her cheeks and said in a honey-laced voice, "I was just fatigued from the drive and sightseeing."

His deep laugh caressed her skin with its musical resonance. "I must say, the sightseeing last night can't be beat," he told her wickedly. "Although it was exhausting, it was quite exhilarating."

"You didn't look too alive this morning when I got up," Audra retorted, trying to move her neck out of reach of nipping teeth, which were causing goose bumps to travel rapidly over her whole exposed body.

"Just getting my beauty sleep and recuperating some of my lost energy," he told her softly.

"That's right. I noticed you ran out of steam at the end," Audra said, her eyes bright with laughter.

Grant curved one arm about her waist and the other around her shoulders. "Are you questioning my staying power?" he growled.

Audra laughed, the tension inside her ready to snap. "All I know is that you seemed awful sleepy for a while there . . ."

Her last word ended in a squeal as Grant pushed her back into the tub, his body joining hers and forcing a deluge of water over the sides. Audra tried to push him off, but he covered her body with his own, tangling his legs with hers, carefully keeping her head out of the now shallow water. "We'll see who has staying power now," he warned, lights dancing in his darkened eyes.

Bracing an elbow on the side of the white bathtub, he arched Audra's body toward him with his other arm. Audra could feel his unmistakable sign of arousal against her thigh, and lambent flames began licking at her body. He trailed his lips from her forehead to her upturned nose, then to her chin and throat, and finally lowered himself to gain access to her breasts. At the small demensions of the tub, he swore briefly, eliciting helpless laughter from Audra at the contortions his large body was forced into.

Grant bit gently at the firm mounds underneath the water, then took each budding nipple into his mouth in turn, circling and lashing at them with his tongue until they were throbbingly erect. Raising her into a half-sitting position, he pressed wet kisses on her midriff, then invaded her navel with quick, hot stabs of his tongue.

Audra could only clutch at his shoulders, her legs moving feverishly in the water, her moans seeming to incite him to greater heights.

Finally, when she thought she could stand no more, he straightened and rose, and stepping out of the tub, he lifted her wet, slippery body and carried her into the bedroom.

Depositing her carefully on the rumpled sheets, Grant followed her down. Audra could not wait any longer. She twined her arms about his neck and pulled him closer, eagerly awaiting his possession. He positioned himself above her and remained poised for a moment, his eyes burning into hers, and then lowered himself gently. He set a slow rhythm, ignoring her cries and her body writhing seductively beneath him. Audra felt the tremors begin deep within her stomach and radiate outward as Grant grabbed her hips and increased the pace of his movements. She scraped her nails across his smooth back and muscular buttocks and felt the tremors increase and multiply, her moans intermingled with his gasps of pleasure at her touch. Then her body became a cauldron of heat, the volcano of her emotions exploding into sensual brilliance as Grant guided her to unknown heights, and after a blistering plateau, slowly descended amidst aftershocks.

Audra whispered his name achingly, holding on to his body as the one stable thing in a whirlwind of sensation. Grant's hands still pressed her to him as she basked in the afterglow and her breathing and pulse decelerated.

Still joined to her, Grant rolled to one side and pulled her with him, cradling her head on one of his arms and gentling her flesh with soothing, tender motions from shoulder to thigh. Bending his head, he dropped a short, hard kiss on her moist lips.

His eyes still held flickering fires when he asked her with a lazy smile, "Any more objections?"

"Oh, I never objected." Audra smiled back, her eyes twinkling audaciously. "But it is too early to tell, don't you think?"

She saw shocked surprise cross his features before a lusty chuckle emerged from the strong, tanned throat, and he rolled her on top of him, parting her lips with a sweeping mastery that enflamed her smoldering senses and ignited once more the fiery core of her being so long suppressed.

- 9 -

LATE INTO THE afternoon, Audra stood next to Grant atop the five-hundred-foot quartzite and sandstone bluffs surrounding Devil's Lake. The fathomless spring-fed lake shone like a jewel before them, and exclamations of delight could be heard from fellow climbers as they contemplated the view.

Grant kept his arm about her waist as he guided Audra to a protruding boulder which gave her the illusion of being suspended in the pure, sun-heated air. He pulled her against him on the narrow white stone, fitting her spine to the width of his chest, and Audra enjoyed the quiet contentment and relaxation after their hectic day.

They had gotten up well after ten, and after a quick lunch at the motel restaurant, had taken the Dells boat ride. It had been a beautiful day, but a bit on the warm side for the long walks interspersed with the scenic stops made by their cruiser. Grant had had trouble negotiating some of the tighter rock formations nature had designed, and Audra had teased him unmercifully about his broad shoulders. When they stopped off at a cafeteria in one of the little islands after traversing a suspended bridge on the last leg of their journey, Audra had suggested they make the climb. She still remembered exploring the different rock formations as a child—often earning a well-deserved spanking when she ventured too far out onto her favorites, like Devil's Doorway, Balance Rock, Cleopatra's Needle—and she had wanted to share them with Grant.

Now, as they enjoyed the cool breeze whipping their moist faces, Audra asked him, "Glad you came?" Grant had not been too enthusiastic about climbing; he'd wanted to spend the rest of the day alone with Audra.

His arm tightened around the midriff bared by her green halter, and he breathed into her ear, "The view is breathtaking, but I'd rather have my breath taken away by other natural beauties."

"Abstinence is good for the soul," Audra said cheekily.

"I'll remind you of that tonight," he promised.

"Well, I was thinking of resting after all the strenuous activities of the past few days," Audra teased him with a serious expression. "You can drop me off at camp before you go back to your motel, and we can both—recharge our batteries, so to speak."

He dropped a kiss on the tip of her pink nose and grinned wolfishly. "Not a chance. Our time here is too limited for us to spend it apart."

"You were quite willing for us to spend our nights apart before," charged Audra, twisting around to face him.

Grant's arm tightened protectively, and he answered readily, "That was before you made up your mind. I didn't want just a body in my bed. I had to be sure you wanted me, not a substitute for your dead husband."

Audra's eyes widened. "You really thought I was replacing Jimmy with you?"

Grant's smile held a tinge of bitterness. "Seduction isn't my scene. When I see something I want, I go after it. But I don't want to stand in for anyone, or have to convince a woman to let me make love to her."

"But don't men view women as challenges to be conquered, as sex objects, if you will?" Audra asked with serious interest.

"It depends on the man. If a man holds a basic contempt for women, he'll view them as objects." His eyes smiled down at her with blue-green fire. "But I had what is nowadays considered an enlightened rearing. I appreciate women and I appreciate sex, and to me the combination is terrific."

Audra grinned impishly, thinking Grant would make a terrific lawyer. "What about women viewing you as a sex object?"

Grant's glance became intent. "Women in general, or you in particular?"

Audra shrugged her shoulders. "Does it matter?"

His features hardened, but so fleeting was the change Audra thought she'd imagined it. "Yes. It does matter. Some relationships are viewed as one-night stands from the very beginning. Others develop into something more significant."

"And I fall into the latter?" Audra asked curiously.

"I don't really take off work on such short notice to follow a green-eyed kitten every week," he told her, an odd note entering his voice. "But to get back to your question. How do you see me?"

Audra thought for a moment, absently placing her

hand on his thigh, and was surprised at the way his flesh contracted under the tight-fitting jeans. "I hadn't given it much thought," she lied, not ready to come to grips with how she *really* felt about him. Certainly not ready to tell him anything at this point. "I just recognized a lot of what you'd said was true and decided to take your advice and start living again."

"And I was the handiest male around?" he asked, and Audra felt his body tense.

"Not exactly." She laughed uncertainly, thinking that perhaps she had razored his male ego. "There is a definite chemistry between us. I've dated a few men since Jimmy's death, but I never wanted to go to bed with any of them."

"Then I'm to feel honored," Grant said mockingly, but Audra had the distinct impression his mockery was self-directed.

Puzzled, she asked him, "Does it bother you?"

"The possibility of the shoe being on the other foot?" He rose and pulled her up with him. "I must say it's somewhat of a novelty. But no, it doesn't bother me."

Audra thought she detected a false note in his voice, but the moment to speak was lost as they made way in the narrow trail for a tour guide and his group, who listened enthusiastically as the naturalist described the flora and geology of the bluffs.

Recalling what he'd said about his profession, she teased him, "I'm really lucky. I get to have an expert with me amidst all these cliffs. How about telling me something about the beginnings of all these gorgeous formations?"

Grant smiled, his somber mood apparently gone for the moment. "I thought you were the tour guide around here," he retorted, putting his hand around her shoulder and bringing her against him. They cut diagonally across the thickly forested top to reach the other side of the hill, escaping some of the lingering heat and avoiding the rest of the climbers making their way down.

"Oh, I only have interesting facts at my fingertips, like the stories about the raftsmen and the Mound Builders, and only some superficial facts about the rocks themselves," she said, twitching her sun-burned nose at him. "But I thought it'd be good for me to acquire some exposure to the bone-dry facts you have at your disposal."

Grant stopped suddenly and pushed her into a thick green alcove. "I'll give you exposure."

Audra laughingly tried to fight him off, but he cornered her against a large tree and placed his hands on either side of her face. Crying in mock alarm, Audra ducked, but Grant lowered his hands instantly, putting them on each side of her torso, his knuckles rubbing the sides of her breasts.

"Grant, please. Someone could come by at any moment," Audra said as she looked anxiously around.

"Don't worry so much, Audra." Grant gave her a smile that did not reassure, and his next words were even less comforting. "We'll hear them trampling in the brush."

Audra tugged at his arms, feeling their heat scorch her skin through the light material of her brief top. "But it might be too late by then," she told him in a tone meant to be reasonable but which emerged as a plea.

Grant threw his head back and laughed, and Audra was reminded of that first time in the library.

"Do you really think I'd take you here, in plain sight of anyone who might happen along?" His tone held censure and—it almost seemed to Audra—hurt.

She looked at him, suddenly unsure, and said, "Well, you just seemed to—I just thought . . ."

"Did I really scare you just now?" he asked gently, brushing away wisps of hair from her moist forehead.

"No, not really scare. I know I'm certainly not immune to your lovemaking, but—"

"But you thought I'd just throw you to the ground and take you." Audra was certain she heard reproof in his voice. When he turned away from her, wearily massaging his neck, she couldn't bear it.

Placing a tentative hand on his shoulder, she was about to apologize when he turned around and, seeing her expression, put his fingers over her lips. "No, don't. I see you haven't learned to trust me totally and perhaps it's my fault, for not making things clearer." Audra kissed the fingers resting on her mouth and let the tip of her tongue play over their callused strength. Grant made a strangled noise, and he slid his hand into her hair, pulling it back to kiss the vulnerable, pulsating curve of her neck.

Audra felt the weakness assailing her legs, and her arms came up, encircling his waist for support. She found herself falling backward, but Grant's other arm was round her shoulder to cushion her back from the jagged bark of the tree. His lips slowly ascended, robbing Audra of conscious thought and then of her breath as he covered her lips with his own, and after tasting their velvety softness, penetrated the dark, warm depths.

"Give me credit for some control, Audra," Grant chided her gently as he removed his mouth—temporarily. His leg parted her thighs, and Audra arched voluptuously, her legs brushing the rough bark, her senses picking up the distant chirping of a bird, the buzzing of bees, the sweet perfume of wild flowers. She became lost in a vortex of sensation, responsive only to the hand that through her halter caressed the fullness of her breast and the lips that were again drinking from hers as if from wild honey.

When Grant ended the embrace, Audra could only stare at him helplessly, her spinning mind unable to comprehend her total response to a man she'd only known for days.

Grant held her gaze with his own and told her quietly, "I don't ever want you to feel afraid of me. I'd never do anything to hurt you—or expose you to others."

Audra nodded, her eyes recognizing the sincerity in his. He hugged her briefly and tightly and then guided her over a large dead trunk as they resumed their leisurely hike.

"You mentioned something about Mound Builders?" he asked casually, his arm draped again companionably over her shoulders.

"They were the earliest people known to have inhabited this region," Audra answered, glad to relieve the intensity of the past few minutes. "They were a very advanced civilization, skilled in the use of copper, which they melted and fashioned into utensils, weapons, and jewelry." Audra paused as Grant jumped over a large rock in their path and then curled his fingers into her waist to lift her over the obstacle. "They're most famous, though, for their creation of strange formations built of earth in the shape of birds, animals, and reptiles. Thousands of these mounds, which are several feet high, were built, and the best examples of them in this area are the Kingsley Bend Indian Mounds, about three miles east of Wisconsin Dells."

"You really are turned on by the past, aren't you?"

Grant asked, smiling, but Audra felt there was more to the question than its superficial query.

So she answered defensively, "I happen to think we can only build a future on what our past has been."

She could see Grant did not agree by the set cast of his features, but he was obviously not going to refute her statement. She knew what he was thinking: that she was clinging to her own past. She kicked a small pebble in her path, sending it flying a few feet in front of her, trying to work off her irritation.

"You look deliciously attractive when you start talking about something that interests you," Grant told her with a teasing smile, but his voice was husky and his eyes were making love to her. "I like to see your cheeks flush, your eyes glowing emerald, your—"

Feeling her indignation begin to melt at his hot glance and words, she snapped, "That's enough."

She thought helplessly, torn between irritation and attraction, that he seemed to be able to divorce himself from everything when he was with her. And although she was glad to have his undivided attention, it was somewhat disconcerting to be constantly under sensual attack. Especially when she was not sure of her real feelings—and she was so susceptible to him.

"Come on," Grant coaxed, unsuccessfully trying to hide the grin curving the firm male lips. "You can't deny a man a little pleasure, can you?"

"I can, and I will," Audra said stubbornly, feeling threatened by his total power over her.

Grant humored her, walking silently by her side for a while, not touching her until she stumbled against a stone hidden in the mossy growth.

Sure he was silently laughing at her, and not blaming

him, she pulled her arm away angrily, but Grant curved his hand around her waist, and although she tried to squirm away, his steel fingers remained in place. After a brief struggle, she let the pleasurable warmth hug her waist, reasoning that there was no need for her to risk a skinned knee if she could avoid it.

Grant didn't attempt to pull her closer to his side, though, and they walked for a few minutes in silence. They had now emerged onto the other side of the hill, and he asked, "Want to hear about some dry, dull facts now?"

Audra ignored the laughter audible in his voice and shrugged with faked disinterest. "Sure, why not."

Grant led her to a huge rock, and when she was sitting down, said slowly, "Let's see..." Rubbing his chin thoughtfully, he stood at an angle from her, looking into the blue distance for a moment.

Framed against the blunt, white cliffs surrounding him, his black hair haloing his tanned face with raven shine, Grant looked achingly irresistible. Audra swallowed painfully, realizing that there was a lot more than sexual attraction in what she felt for Grant. Or could it be that this magnetism and sensual power over her were so great she had lost all sense of proportion?

He turned around and Audra jumped guiltily, as if caught with her hand in the cookie jar. His deep, flowing voice mesmerized her, and she found she could not take her eyes from his profile as he rested one foot atop a flat stone and his arm across his knee.

"The Great Lakes as we know them are mere Johnny-come-latelies when you measure them in the whole scheme of things, the earth's long and lumbering evolution. Five hundred million years ago, before the start of our modern geological time, the area was inundated by molten lava erupting from the core of the earth. Then came water and periods of flooding and draining, until a short time ago—a million years—when glaciers arrived from the north." He stopped, seeking Audra's reaction. "Bored to tears yet?"

"No, not at all," Audra negated. Content to look at him in the fading sun, she would have been happy to hear him recite the multiplication tables at the moment.

His deep voice resumed his narration, and Audra felt an inner thrill at its pleasing timbre. "As the glacial age retreated and the havoc ceased, plant and animal life came back into the area. Fossilized remains of mammoths, whales, and mastodons have been found, prehistoric monsters that have been carbon-dated as having lived in the Great Lakes regions as recently as ten thousand years ago or less."

"Incredible, isn't it?" Audra looked about her as she visualized that long-ago time that had always fascinated her.

"There's a number of theories on the exact creation of the Great Lakes," Grant continued as he straightened and came to sit by her, "from one that holds that they were formed by a series of earthquakes, to one identifying the culprit as an ancient river system which is far older than the ice ages. The last of them, as a matter of fact, was named the Wisconsin by geologists, because the southern reach of the ice flow is paralled by the state's southern border."

"Learn something new every day." Audra smiled, her earlier displeasure gone, but some of her uneasiness remaining.

Grant seemed to sense it, and he ran his hand soothingly through her thick hair, which the hot sun had turned tawny in just a few days.

"What are you thinking?" he asked her quietly after a while.

Audra sighed and answered half truthfully. "Oh, about the times I used to come up here with my parents. When I graduated high school they gave me the gold tent as a present, and five of my friends and I used to come every chance we got." She added softly, "I stopped after my first semester in college, which is too bad. Jimmy would have loved it here."

His hand stiffened in her hair for a moment and then continued its stroking movement. Audra noticed it, and turned to look at him, asking, "It doesn't bother you if I talk about Jimmy, does it? He is part of my past, one I'm just now really coming to terms with."

Grant scanned her face, almost, Audra thought, as if he were searching for something. "No, not really. I'm greedy, and want all of your attention. No man wants the woman he desires thinking about another man, even if he is dead."

Before Audra could make any sort of response, he swopped down and picked her up, rising with her in his arms. Walking a few yards, he dropped quick kisses on her bare shoulder and, letting her slide down, told her, "Let's go. It's almost dark now, and we still have about three hundred feet to go."

Audra tagged reluctantly, hating to leave things hanging in the air unresolved. And yet did she have the right to question him deeper? After all, he had only claimed to desire her. Not love her. After this brief, passionate interlude, they would both go their separate ways. Audra frowned, realizing she did not like the idea of a future without Grant. Already he had become imbedded in her mind . . . her body . . . her thoughts . . .

Preoccupied with her musing, she payed no attention to the uneven ground and stumbled over an upturned tree root. Although she tried to save herself, she fell hard on her derriere and slid down several mossy stones, bouncing helplessly before coming to a painfully abrupt stop on an angular rock. Grant, who had been slightly ahead of her in the narrow trail that allowed passage for only one person at a time, was beside her in an instant.

His worried expression put her own pain in the background, and she instinctively put out an unsteady hand to reassure Grant, saying unevenly, "I'm okay. Just some bruises and abrasions, luckily where they won't show."

Audra tried to make a joke of it, but felt the muscles in his forearm cord beneath her fingers, and then his hands were roving carefully over her body, checking torso, arms, and legs as he twisted her this way and that to make sure there was nothing broken.

His black eyebrows came together as he noticed the deep gash bleeding profusely in the back of her right thigh, where the jagged edge of a rock had cut into her. He lifted the cuff of her brief black shorts and told her roughly, "Hold it up while I put a compress on it."

Audra remained lying on her side, bracing herself on her left elbow while he took a clean handkerchief from his back jeans pocket and held it to the wound for a while with steady pressure. Telling Audra to keep pressing on it, he took off his red shirt and ripped the hem off, wrapping it about her thigh to hold the handkerchief in place. Audra looked at its neat, efficient appearance and complimented him, "You'd make a good nurse."

"I'd rather play doctor when I get you back to the motel," he bit out, a nasty glint in his eyes. "That is, if we manage to get you back in one piece."

Audra didn't understand why he was so angry. After all, it was she who had fallen, and she blinked back tears as the pain she'd tried so hard to hide began throbbing in her cuts and throughout her aching body. Angry herself now, she said almost petulantly, "I don't know why you're so upset. *I* was the one who took the jolt, not you."

"Don't you think I know that?" he barked, a dangerous glint turning his eyes a metallic blue. "You don't know the scare you gave me when I heard you cry out and saw you bouncing like a ball out of control on those jagged rocks, not able to get to you in time. You could have cut your head on one of those sharp stones, and you wouldn't be here to give me lip."

"Give you lip! Why, you overbearing, rude, inconsiderate lout," Audra screamed. "The least you could do is show some sympathy and understanding."

"My understanding right now extends to not swatting that already abused bottom for not sticking close to me so that I could have absorbed your fall with my body," he told her icily.

"You dare lay a hand on me and it's the last time you ever touch me," Audra warned, her voice choked with the emotion of her convictions.

Grant dropped on his haunches next to her, his eyes level with hers, his face sobering as he saw the light of battle in her face. "I believe you mean that," he said slowly, wonderingly.

"You bet I do," Audra said forcefully. "Men might

be physically stronger, but I would never respect a man who traded on that strength to show his superiority or keep a woman *in line*."

Grant looked at her intently and smiled suddenly, his eyes growing a light blue-green. "You're right. I wouldn't respect a man much either in that case. I guess I should change that to get my hands on your lovely throat and choke some sense into you." His eyes danced with amusement, and his voice changed to a lighter tone. "Think that would be less chauvinistic?"

Audra smiled in return, knowing that Grant understood what she'd meant and—more importantly—had respected her position. "Considering it takes that faintly patronizing, paternalistic edge off, I'd say yes." Walking her fingers up his bare chest from his belt buckle to his neck, where she made a squeezing motion, she added sweetly. "And considering I feel the same urge to do that to you many times, I think it's a fair description of affairs."

Grant grinned, his teeth flashing white in the swiftly falling darkness. "Then we can both put our hands on each other's necks tonight," he said wickedly, and Audra felt warmth rush into her face. She didn't need him to remind her that the last time they'd made love together she had almost crushed the breath out of him.

"We should get going," she mumbled hastily.

Audra could almost feel his amused glance on her flesh, but she ignored him, averting her face while he carried her for a few minutes down the narrow path, then put her down when the trail became wider, keeping his arm about her waist and fairly lifting her off her feet as they negotiated the quickest descent possible under the circumstances.

- *10* -

AUDRA RELAXED UNDER Grant's ministering hands, the cream he was massaging into her skin marvelously soothing to her all-pervading aches and pains. Since she had taken a hot bath and gotten into bed, Audra had discovered muscles previously unknown to her and had flinched as she'd made the long trek from bathroom to bed. Audra knew that the rushing of the past few days, the exertions from the boat ride and hike of the trails, and the climb that afternoon had all combined to make her one big ache. When Grant had returned from town with fresh dressings and that awful-smelling liniment, she had tried to ignore him and keep her body covered with the cool white sheets. But Grant had won the tug-of-war and had uncaringly rolled her onto her stomach, taking care of her cuts and spreading that awful cream all over her cringing, protesting flesh.

Her accusations that something so vile could have no

recuperative powers had gone unheeded as Grant had mercilessly kneaded her arms, legs, and back, paying particular attention to her derriere. Audra had accused him of experiencing sick, perverse joy at inflicting pain on her, and he'd laughingly replied that he was just treating her as he would a horse, and since the cream had been donated by the town's vet, he was just acting accordingly.

That had effectively shut her up—partly because after the first few excruciating minutes, which had brought tears rolling down sunburned cheeks, she had begun feeling exquisite relief, and partly because her tired mind had sluggishly started seeking ways to extract suitable retribution.

Grant turned her onto her back, and this time his hands were a lot gentler as they slowly rubbed her body. Audra tried her best to remain unfeeling under fingers that were demanding a response from her. She began counting sheep, multiplying and dividing, absently registering that Grant had changed his shirt to a denim one before going out to get the liniment. She noticed with exhausted detachment that his breathing had begun to quicken, and his fingers trembled as they massaged a calf, then worked tantalizingly up her leg to the thigh, and repeated the process with the other leg. His hands sought the curves of her hips and the hollow of her stomach, tenderly stroking her skin. Audra saw the light of passion in his turbulent blue glance as the intensity of his caresses magnified, and a fleeting smile softened the determined curve of her lips the second before she fell asleep, her last conscious thought that she had hit upon the perfect instrument of revenge.

* * *

When Audra woke up, she found to her pleased surprise that her body seemed to be almost completely recovered. With the exception of her coccyx bone and the still throbbing cut in the back of her thigh, her aches had all pretty much receded. She missed Grant's body next to hers and frowned, puzzled that she received no answer when she called his name.

She'd awoken once during the night to find her body fitting into Grant's with warm comfort, and at her slight movement, his arm had pulled her closer to him, as if preventing her, even in sleep, from moving away. Audra had had no such intention and had merely attempted to shift her leg, which had fallen asleep under the heavy weight of Grant's thigh. After finding an eased position, she had contentedly curled deeper into his arms, falling asleep again promptly.

She had not been aware of Grant getting up this morning; he must have been very careful to disentangle their bodies without waking her. After calling his name a second time and securing no response, Audra lifted her legs slowly over the side of the bed and spotted the note propped on the night table. It read, "Didn't want to wake you up, so I went out to breakfast. Will be back shortly, sleepyhead. Grant."

Audra had just finished showering, spending extra time lathering and rinsing away the marvelous cream and changing her dressing, when she heard a key turn in the lock. Wrapping a large white towel around her, she entered the bedroom and saw Grant come into the room, carrying a brown paper bag. He greeted her with a smile and dropped a kiss on her cheek. "Brought some clothes for you. Thought you'd prefer not to get into the ragged, dusty remains from yesterday."

Touched by his thoughtfulness and slightly hesitant about last night, Audra began looking through the bag, finding a one-piece maroon terry suit, her wedgies, tennis shoes, her one-piece bathing suit, and lace bikini panties. "No bra?" she asked questioningly.

"My kindness doesn't extend that far," Grant grinned, grabbing her hand and pulling her onto his lap as he sat down on the mock-leather chair.

Audra let out a cry, her bottom tender as it brushed against the iron bone of Grant's knee. "Sorry," he smiled, shifting her higher onto his lap so that she could sit on the relatively softer flesh of his muscular thighs.

She noticed he had on navy slacks and shirt and a white jacket. "Going somewhere?" she asked curiously.

"Just had to take care of some business," he said, his eyes twinkling. Audra frowned, not liking his smug expression, but he continued, "I received a call from my general manager while I was out this morning. It seems a crisis has arisen, and the motel owner took a message. I told him not to put through any calls while I was gone."

Audra remembered seeing the manager yesterday when they got back, his eyes speculative and interested as they had rested on her figure. She flushed, thinking he would be having a field day now, and resolved not to come back to Grant's motel. What seemed so right in the tent, and under the canopy of blue skies and trees—even that first night—became somewhat tinged when viewed by prying, speculative eyes.

She noticed Grant was observing the change of expression on her mobile face with a slight frown and asked quietly, "Do you have to go back, then?"

Grant shook his head. "No, not unless they find they can't get on top of things. I handpicked my top executives for their innovative, take-charge attitudes. Since I'm often gone on overseas assignments, I have to be sure I can depend on them." He playfully loosened the fold on her towel, and Audra automatically clutched it to prevent it from sliding open. "I just have to make a few long-distance calls. It shouldn't take more than two, three hours."

When Audra would not give up possession of the towel, he brushed his lips slightly back and forth on one very pink shoulder. "You don't seem to tan very well, do you," he said, letting his tongue sneak out as he turned his concentration to the hollow between her breasts.

Audra felt her breasts swelling from the fleeting caress and took a deep breath. "No, as a matter of fact I don't. I usually turn a coral pink or bright red and then go back to white again. Luckily, I don't peel easily, either."

Grant moved his head sideways, and keeping one arm circling her waist, he lifted her arm with his left hand and trailed kisses in a downward sensuous path until he reached his objective. Then he began stroking her inner elbow, dampening the sensitive skin with the erotic movements of his tongue. Audra felt her flesh erupt into thousands of little goose bumps and found she could no longer remain passive. She opened his shirt with clumsy fingers, and when the last button was disposed of, bent her own head to kiss the furry, muscular male chest. Excited by the bristling sensation of his hair against her lips, Audra felt the need to taste him too, and her own tongue began tiny circling motions from shoulder to shoulder. When the wet tip, sensitized by the ripple of muscle and tingle of rough hair, reached a male nipple, licking it into hard arousal, Audra felt Grant's unequivocal response against her hip. His teeth dug into her shoulder for a sharp moment before he placed a kiss on it and raised his head, his breathing irregular and his face darkly flushed.

"I think I'd better put a stop to this right now or I won't be able to go make those phone calls," he joked, but Audra saw by the rigid set of his body and the muscle moving in his cheek that he was exercising tremendous will power as he picked her up and got up with her in his arms, carrying her to the bed, where he set her down carefully. Audra felt a thrilling sense of satisfaction at the knowledge that she was able to incite him to such heated passion, as he had done with her so often.

Audra couldn't let him go without clearing up last night's situation, and she waited until he rebuttoned his shirt with sure, deft fingers and tucked the shirt back into the dark pants before she spoke.

"Grant, about last night." His eyes flew to hers, and Audra sustained his brilliant blue gaze unflinchingly. "I didn't mean to go to sleep on you."

Grant looked at her quizzically, and his words expressed his doubt. "That beatific smile of yours didn't seem to express too much sorrow at the prospect."

Audra colored, knowing that although she'd not actually sought sleep, she had enjoyed the small revenge. "Well, I was glad about paying you back for your rough treatment earlier," she told him softly. "But it was only intended to make you suffer a bit."

Grant caressed her cheek, smiling ruefully. "You succeeded admirably. But it doesn't matter, one way or the other. I was punishing you last night for the fright you gave me. His eyes darkened, and Audra recalled the sharp, cutting pain and endless bouncing. "But since you took such punitive measures last night, I feel you owe me one, and I intend collecting tonight."

Audra smiled back, liking the way he didn't hold grudges. As a matter of fact, she told herself as she picked up her clothes from the bed, she was beginning to like more and more things about Grant Williams.

Rising and intending to go to the bathroom to change, she found her way blocked by Grant, who put a detaining hand on her hip.

"Where do you think you're going?" he asked softly.

"To change, of course. I don't intend to stay here all morning."

"I'll take you down to the beach and join you as soon as I can," Grant agreed. "But," he added quietly, "there's no need to leave the room to get dressed. I thought we'd progressed beyond that."

The seductive power of his words ignited something deep inside her body. Grant read the confusion and desire that must have been in her eyes, and he gently pulled the towel away from her, his darkened glance devouring the slim white body with its bands of pink, the high, proud breasts moving rapidly to the tune of her heartbeat, and the smooth stomach which contracted under the force of the blue-green gaze, the long, shapely legs that trembled from the sensations he'd aroused in her body with his sensuous scrutiny.

Grant embraced her with possessive tenderness, molding her to the hard shape of his body, running his hands delicately over the heated skin of her back, waist, buttocks, thighs. He whispered in her ear with a voice that was slightly unsteady, "I want you, Audra. I enjoy making love to you. But I also like to look at you, feel you, caress you." He raised a hand and lifted her chin, looking deeply into her eyes. "Do you see why you had nothing to fear atop Devil's Lake?"

Audra nodded, unable to speak. She saw his eyes lower to her mouth and closed her eyes as the exquisite sensation of the feathery kiss coursed slowly through her body, filling it with warmth and joy. When he lifted his head again, she was reluctant to open her eyes and leave the dream world that enveloped her in silky, sensuous threads.

Grant sighed deeply and moved her away from him, to pick up her panties. The black lace tickled seductively as he kneeled and pulled the panties up over her thighs, dropping a kiss on her navel before handing her the maroon romper outfit.

Having readjusted to reality somewhat, Audra smiled as he zippered the terry outfit and told him with laughter in her voice, "I'd say this is something of a switch. You make as good a dresser as undresser."

Her teasing brought out the green glints in his eyes, and he smiled as she put on her wedgies. "No more torture, please. I have to make those phone calls. Once I make sure the duties I delegated are being carried out and the crisis is in hand, I'll join you. It's going to be quite long as it is, without the memory of this luscious body and your unfair teasing."

Audra sat on the bed, leaned back on her extended hands, and looked up at Grant seductively. "It seems to me you're the one keeping us apart. I have all day."

Grant groaned and pulled her up with one swift, savage movement. "You, woman, are going to pay tonight," he growled, tickling her neck and throat until she laughingly begged for mercy. Keeping one arm around her waist, he collected her belongings with the other and half carried, half dragged a protesting Audra out the door.

The light, joyous mood carried them back to camp, and Grant dropped Audra off by the registration office. The lake gleamed sapphire in the late morning sun, and Audra was filled with anticipation at the thought of swimming in the clear, cool water after buying some rolls at the small store.

Kissing Grant goodybe, she deliberately prolonged the brief kiss he'd dropped on her lips by parting them and licking his with the tip of her tongue. Grant crushed her into a bone-breaking embrace and deepened the kiss most satisfactorily, with a moan that came from deep within his body. When he finally pushed her from him almost violently again, he said with dangerous softness, "You're playing with fire, kitten. Be careful you don't get burned."

Audra's laugh filled the plush white interior as she grabbed the bag and climbed out of the car. She called back gaily, before running lightly down to the beach, "Seems to me you're the one in danger of being incinerated."

She saw the storm that clouded Grant's expression, but calmly ignored it as she waved at him saucily. It felt terribly wonderful to be getting her own back, and seeing Grant so consumed with desire for her filled her with intense satisfaction.

The sight of sparkling blue water on all four sides, with the white, gray, and red-brown cliffs thrusting jaggedly into the azure firmament, made Audra sigh with pleasure. She looked down at the two boys sprawled on the other side of the small row boat and smiled in amusement. It had taken them almost an hour to get to the center of the large lake, and the silver boat had looked like a big, awkward bug which had lost its sense of direction as it had zig-zagged its way across.

Audra had met Kevin and Ryan on the beach, and when she'd asked about their parents, she'd been told Heather, husband, and baby Erin had gone into Baraboo a short while ago. They'd also said they'd been swimming most of the morning and were tired of waiting for their dad to come back from shopping to take them rowing.

The expectant, hopeful look on their faces as they recounted their tales of woe had been enough to melt the hardest heart. Audra, who adored children, had been a pushover. Ruffling the two red pelts of hair, Audra had told them she'd take them and had covered her ears at the wild whoops of joy.

Now, after battling the small metal boat for nearly an hour—they'd insisted they wanted to "steer"—both of them were exhausted, and Audra looked with affectionate humor at the small boys whose hair exactly matched the color of their lifejackets. Keeping a straight face, she asked peppily, "Ready to go back, boys? We can't float in the middle of the lake all day. Your parents will be back before too long and we don't want to worry them, do we?"

Two pairs of identical green eyes looked dazedly back at her, and their grunts indicated that not much was of vital importance at the moment.

Hiding a smile, Audra asked casually, "Mind if I row us back? You did such a good job getting us here that I feel I haven't pulled my weight."

The green eyes showed marked interest all of a sudden, and Kevin said magnanimously, "Sure, go ahead. Just holler if you need any help."

Audra thanked him gravely for his offer and began the return trip at snail's pace, the muscles of her arms and legs welcoming the exercise. Her derriere still stung, but Audra gritted her teeth and purposely slowed her rowing to delay arriving at the beach in a short time, which would have embarrassed the boys' first efforts.

Both boys jumped out to push the boat to shore—which to Audra had never before looked so welcome—and gallantly helped her out of it. Their energies once again restored, they decided to play with the beach ball, and Audra sighed as she looked down at her still dry gold maillot ruefully. She had not gotten a chance to go swimming yet, but could not ignore the appeal in the freckled faces.

The boys proved tireless at the game, and finally Audra collapsed on the sand, refusing to get up again and naming them the victors.

But the boys were not ready to rest and began scooping up sand, covering her tired, damp body with the grainy, itchy stuff. She brushed it off her body with quick motions, but the four little hands were even faster, swiftly and noisily shoveling the sand on top of her and making a slim, curved shape of Audra where only her head was showing. Audra had by now given up, thinking that once they had her totally blanketed, they might leave her alone and entertain themselves.

But a shower of sand suddenly hit her face, and Audra squealed in outrage. "Not in the face," she cried, and prepared to sit up and do battle, when a large shadow fell over her. She twisted her head, spitting some grains out of her dry mouth, and saw Grant towering over her, his bronzed body clad in brief, white swimming trunks, holding a wriggling body under each arm.

"Having trouble with these two baby sharks?" he asked, his teeth flashing white against the deep tan.

Audra smiled back, sure that her pleasure at seeing him was reflected in her eyes. "As a matter of fact, yes. I'm waiting for their parents to get back, but I'm thinking that perhaps they'll be glad if we get rid of them. What do you think?"

Grant appeared to consider her question and then answered severely, "I think you're right. Mean fish should be thrown back where they belong—into the water." Securing his hold on the kicking, squirming boys, he winked at her and turned, heading for the lake.

Audra raised her head to follow his progress, enjoying the play of muscles in his back as he restrained the struggles of the boys and the powerful strength of his thighs as he walked securely in the sand, easily supporting the additional weight.

She watched as Grant lifted the boys high in the air, dropped them in thigh-high water, and then proceeded to dunk them several times. She smiled tenderly as she saw how he let his body be pulled down under the combined attack of the shrieking boys, closing her eyes when she saw that it soon developed into a free-for-all.

Audra found herself wondering drowsily how Grant would be with his own children. He obviously had the patience, the gentle firmness, and seemed to understand them quite well...

She sat up abruptly at the direction her thoughts were taking. She couldn't let herself think of Grant in those terms. And yet, she'd already started.... Putting her arms about her drawn-up knees, Audra tried to keep out the chill that invaded her at the thought that she might be becoming too involved with Grant.

And she couldn't allow that to happen. She felt panicky and confused. She remembered the pain she had felt during the months after Jimmy's death and how she had wished at the time that they had not waited to have children. But she had come to terms with her loneliness and had realized it had been for the best. It was sheer madness to even think of Grant in those terms. She did not know how he felt about her. . . . She wasn't sure of her own feelings . . .

For the next few minutes, she stared unseeingly at the shimmering lake, its harsh glare making her eyes water, and tried to control her wayward thoughts. The cold began to dissipate slowly, and by the time she lay back down on the hot sand, she had forced her mind to be blank and her body to relax.

- *11* -

AUDRA OPENED HER eyes when she felt drops of cold water disturb her comfortable doze. She wrinkled her nose in irritation and glared up at Grant, who kneeled beside her with a wide grin on his tanned face. She read something in his too-green eyes, and her gaze flew to the hand he was keeping behind his back. Belatedly trying to sit up and remove the weight of settled sand on her body, she was not quick enough and a pail of cold water descended on her face, wetting and clamping her hair on her forehead and riveting in a frigid path down her chin and neck.

She heard the squeals and giggles coming from somewhere beyond her vision and arched her neck to look behind her at the delighted boys jumping up and down at her predicament. Looking at them with mock rage and hiding the smile trying to surface, she asked them in a fierce tone, "I suppose that red pail belongs to you?"

Kevin was quick to deny ownership. "It's Ryan's. I'm too old to make sand castles."

Audra managed to sit up, and Grant helped her to get most of the sand off her body. "Well, I don't think anyone is ever too old to build a castle. Grant here," she said, looking at him impishly, "is actually an expert. And he'll help us build a terrific one. Won't you, Grant?"

Grant's eyes slitted at her suggestion, and he drawled, "My talent extends to many fields. What about making two castles, and we'll see whose is more real looking?"

Both boys eagerly agreed to the challenge, and Ryan teamed with Audra while Kevin and Grant took a spot a few feet away from them on the uncrowded beach.

Audra had Ryan collect tiny branches, stones, and leaves and kept her body between their castle and the opposing team's. After a half hour of frenzied digging, careful constructing, and water carrying to fill the moat surrounding the castle, Audra announced proudly, "Ready!"

Ryan was flushed with happy anticipation, but his face fell as he saw that the castle Grant and Kevin had erected was almost identical in size and shape.

Audra couldn't help the laugh that gurgled to her lips, which became full-throated when Grant said drolly, "Are you finally convinced we are totally compatible?"

She hid her inner shock at the words. Although Grant had meant them jokingly, they hit too close to home and her heart began to race. She turned from him, afraid that he might read the agitated thoughts that had swirled in her mind only moments before, and faced the boys.

Seeing their look of consternation, Audra quickly wiped tears of laughter from her eyes and gained control of herself and her runaway emotions.

"I think we have to declare a tie. Don't you agree, Grant?"

He nodded solemnly and said, "Absolutely. We have two outstanding castles here, and these two young men should be rewarded for their efforts. What do you say to an ice cream, men?"

Their faces brightened instantly, and they readily accompanied Grant to the park store, which carried staples such as milk, bread, and eggs, plus rolls and ice cream.

Audra headed for the lake and for the next few minutes kept a watch for Grant. When he took a long time, she decided to go for a swim; the beach was not overly large, and he could spot her easily.

She was floating on her back, enjoying the relaxing, weightless sensation with the occasional lap of waves playing about her body in smooth, pleasant caresses, when a steel band settled about her waist and pulled her down. Audra opened her eyes in shock and saw Grant's softly distorted face a second before he covered her mouth with his own. He pressed her down to the sandy depths and kept her there for a long, intense moment, his hands pulling down her maillot and caressing her spine and breasts before her fingers tightened on his shoulders to signal her lack of oxygen.

Grant took them up instantly with a powerful kick of his legs. Audra maintained her hold on the bulging muscles of his shoulders while she flung the hair out of her face with a toss of her head. Grant smoothed the brown mass backward with his hand, keeping his other arm about her waist.

He pressed her curves to his unyielding flesh, and Audra felt quicksilver tongues of fire race over her wet skin as his body chased away the coolness of the water and infused his warmth into her own. Audra tried to pull up her bathing suit, but Grant prevented her by molding her body so closely to his that they seemed as of one flesh.

Keeping them afloat by treading water, Grant deliberately brushed his legs against her thighs in a circular movement, and the rough, springy contact further inflamed senses already afire with the feel of her bare breasts crushed against the rippling, furry chest.

Her eyes were lost in the blue-green depths of his when he suddenly turned his head to his left, as an animal sensing prey. The sound began to infiltrate Audra's spinning senses, and she turned her head also, sighting Kevin laboriously swimming to their side.

Grant's hands released their iron grip and deftly pulled her maillot back up, brushing her nipples with branding possession before adjusting it into place. Audra gasped in burning reaction and looked at him reproachfully as Kevin reached them.

"Mom and Dad wanted to know if you'd like to join them for dinner tonight. They're going back to camp now, and they said there's plenty of food. Dad's gonna barbecue."

Audra looked at Grant, wanting to accept the invitation but not sure what he'd think of it.

Grant read the question in her eyes and answered for both of them. "We accept. What time does your mother want us over?"

"She said two hours. Plenty of time to get showered and dressed, she said." He gave them the directions to their campsite and swam in the direction of shore again, his healthy little body kicking with tremendous force and energy.

"That's one little boy who's going to be pooped to-night," Audra said with a tender smile, watching the orange-red head bob up and down away from them.

"Make that two," Grant said, giving her a lazy smile. "Shall we go get ready?"

Audra nodded, shivers of excruciating ecstasy trembling through her at the scorching need in Grant's eyes. Wanting to recover from her swimming senses, she shot forward, noticing Grant keeping up with her with smooth cleaving motions. She strained her body with quick strokes and powerful kicks, hoping to alleviate the answering need of her body.

Audra took the towels, bathing suits, and her maroon outfit from the clothesline, where she'd hung them to dry before leaving for dinner at the Donahues'.

"They're nice, aren't they?" she murmured softly, leaning against one of the trees supporting the clothesline, still holding the dry clothes in her arms.

"Mmmm." Grant moved over to where she stood and braced one arm against the tree trunk. "They seemed to like you a lot too. You have a way with children."

"Look who's talking," Audra teased. "They wanted to thank us both for keeping their 'monsters' entertained."

"Ever thought of having any of your own?" Grant asked casually.

Audra breathed deeply, exhaling the breath slowly. "I did at one time, but as you know, Jimmy had been against it. I've always loved children." Her voice was laced with pain as she added, "I used to think it might have been easier to bear Jimmy's loss—even if I was just a child myself. But it's probably best this way."

Grant rubbed his fingers gently across her cheek and took the clothes from her. "I think it's time we went to bed."

Audra looked into his eyes, and the glittering look enveloped her with warmth. She followed him in silence as he unzipped the tent, and stepped inside carefully. Her fingers sought and found the flashlight on her sleeping bag, and she kept it at chest level, so that it wouldn't blind them.

Closing both zippers, Grant turned around, and his eyes were full of humor. Looking pointedly at the single mattress, he said wryly. "I know this tent sleeps six or seven people, but we seem to have a logistics problem here. Couldn't you have brought a double one?"

Audra arched her brows and retorted, "When I first planned this vacation, it was to be just that—a relaxed, restful, uneventful vacation," she stressed the adjectives. "Now I find I'm even denied sleep at night." Picking up her mint-green pajamas, she walked to a corner of the cabin tent and added, "Of course there is a very simple solution. You could go back to the motel."

"Without you? Not a chance." He moved to her side, ducking his head to avoid hitting the canvas ceiling. "And you won't need these," he added, grabbing her pajamas and tossing them on top of her stacked luggage.

"Is that so?" Audra asked.

His response was to take the flashlight from her and place it on the ground and then to begin unbuttoning her copper-and-jade print blouse and pull it out of her copper pants. Audra stopped him, putting her hands on the sinewy wrists, and told him in a voice gone suddenly husky. "My turn."

She unbuttoned his short-sleeved cream shirt slowly,

sensuously heightening anticipation. As soon as it was opened, she slid it down the broad shoulders, raining tiny kisses on the hair-roughened chest. She unbuckled the leather belt, and sliding the zipper open, dragged the brown pants past the slim male hips. Grant stepped out of them, and Audra's eyes took in the beauty of the hard male body, naked now except for black briefs and summer sandals.

Her gaze returned to Grant's face and concentrated for a heated moment on the firm, sensuous male lips before moving upward to lock with his eyes. She undressed without hurry, aware every second of Grant's glance following her every motion.

When only her skin-colored bra and panties remained, Grant moved forward and picked her up, his mouth meeting hers in a kiss of restrained power. It was as if both tacitly agreed that this time there was to be no rushing— that their passion was to be allowed to grow unhurriedly and be savored slowly.

Grant lowered her onto the fleecy covering, and after following her down, removed the rest of their clothes, asking in a soft murmur, "Are you cold?"

Audra raised her arms and encircled his neck, smiling as she whispered back, "Are you kidding?"

She saw that unnamed emotion cross Grant's chiseled features, but it was swiftly veiled. He cupped her face in his hand and told her, "You have really blossomed these past few days, Audra. Not only have you lost that tired, rushed look, but you've melted that icy shell and have responded like that passionate woman I sensed in the library."

"You would have to bring that up," Audra said, but this time there was no sense of embarrassment.

"How could I ever forget my first glimpse of this delicious body?" he asked, running his hand from her shoulder to thigh in a light, feathery movement.

Audra shivered and pulled his body more closely to hers. "And I remember that you scared me at first. I'd seen you around campus several times and at a couple of the basketball games. I tried to tell myself I was afraid of you because you were a stranger—because I didn't know your name." She raised her head to plant a biting kiss on his neck. "But I know now that it was fear of a different sort—fear of the power you could have over me."

Grant buried his hands in the thick tawny hair, rubbing its gleaming strands between his fingertips. "And I think your friend Mona is somewhat of a matchmaker. I must admit, though, she was a great help, letting me know you were going camping. Perhaps she intended me to go with you," he grinned.

"I wouldn't put it past her. She's been trying to fix me up with someone for the past two years."

"She seems to have succeeded. I'll have to thank her properly when we get back. Although I'd have been waiting for you when you returned, I must thank her for saving me time."

"And you don't like to waste time?" Audra asked with a teasing smile.

The corners of his mouth tilted, and the dark green eyes gleamed. "Think of the waste," he murmured against her throat as his head descended to nuzzle her.

Audra turned her head, seeking his mouth, but although Grant nibbled at her lips and rubbed his mouth teasingly against hers, he did not deepen the kiss to her satisfaction. He began a calculated attack on her senses which left her gasping. His caresses drove her to the brink, and when her arms grasped the rippling muscles of his back, seeking a total possession, he held back, soothing her down and keeping her at a maddening plateau. Audra tried to push him into taking her, her hands caressing him with fiery urgency and her body writhing seductively under his until his breath became irregular and his body rigid with self-control. Grant again took her to the heights, and after withholding possession, caressed her into a sensuous frenzy. "I told you you'd get burned," he said against her hair, his words muffled and husky, his body completely covering hers, stilling her heated struggles.

Audra whispered, "Damn you," in physical and mental frustration, and he laughed in her ear, the deep sound, his warm breath, and the clean male scent all combining to race chills over her entire body as he commanded in a low, rasping voice, "Tell me you want me."

Audra fought the sensual haze enveloping her and tried to make her body obey the dictates of her mind. But Grant renewed his erotic attack, and Audra found her body slipping away from her, spiraling higher in a whirlwind of emotions, and cried, "I want you. Damn you!" before losing consciousness for a moment as wave upon wave of pain-pleasure invaded her body and shook it in continuous convulsions. She felt Grant join her on the scalding trek, his body stiffening at the moment of release, his arms cradling her body as her arms clung desperately to his shoulders. His male gasp mingled with her cries, and he whispered against her damp throat, "I want you, Audra."

It took a very long time, before her body was once again her own.

Grant lay sideways, and he rolled Audra onto her side, his eyes tenderly gazing into her face, covered with curling damp tendrils. He brushed them away, and followed the line of her nose, mouth, and chin with a light touch.

Audra looked at him in annoyance that resurfaced once her breathing and pulse rate were restored to almost normal. "That was a dirty trick you pulled," she accused.

"Dirty?" he questioned dryly. "I'd told you earlier you were playing with fire. There's more than one way to get burned."

Her eyes widened in reproof. "You were teaching me a lesson?"

Grant's voice now showed annoyance. "Don't be childish. I was not teaching you a lesson, merely showing you that teasing can become painful and that desire can cut two ways."

Still incensed, Audra was not in a mood to listen. "All I know is that Jimmy would never have done something like that. He—"

Grant interrupted with sudden fury, his eyes burning with dark fires. "I am not your dead husband. Stop trying to identify me with him. I will not tolerate three persons in our bed."

His head swooped down and claimed hers with barely controlled savagery. Audra did not resist at first, stunned by his violent reaction. Grant had said he didn't like to hear Jimmy mentioned, but she had never thought it would have such a strong effect on him. When she tried to resist his caresses, she found her body betrayed her. She returned his kisses and moved her hands over the strong, hard male body. But when Grant took her this time, Audra found she was giving herself with the same reserve she had felt the first time he had made love to her.

Audra sensed a desperate edge to Grant's possession and marveled that she was not afraid of the tightly leashed violence she sensed in him. His hands and body remained constrained in his fierce, overwhelming act of love.

Grant held her against the curve of his wet body when it was over, and she could feel the anger and rage still boiling near the surface. But he remained silent and Audra didn't speak either, not knowing how to broach the subject.

He lay awake long into the night, and Audra sensed the exact instant he fell asleep. She knew she'd not get any sleep that night, because her thoughts were churning in unresolved turmoil. Audra knew that while Grant might not like to hear about Jimmy, her marriage was a part of her past. It couldn't be erased, and Audra didn't want to erase it.

She saw in hindsight that she'd made some comparative statements about Jimmy and Grant—and wished she could recall her thoughtless words, but she also felt that Grant was at fault for over reacting. He knew she'd been married; he couldn't expect her to block out her past. But he'd acted as if he owned her, and yet he had not told her he loved her—nor that he wanted anything permanent beyond Devil's Lake. With Jimmy she had known where she stood from the beginning.

Audra frowned in the darkness, confused about her own motivations. She realized now that it was more than sexual attraction that bound her to Grant. But could she be sure that she didn't just feel such an overpowering response to him because she had abstained from any close relationships—both physical and emotional—for almost four years? Perhaps she *was* just seeing Grant as a sex object.

And what about Grant? What did *he* really want from her? He had been gentle, caring, affectionate. But to a man of his age and experience, it could be just a pleasant interlude in his life. She was in a helpless quandary. She'd be hurt if he only wanted her for a few days or even weeks. And yet if he meant to develop the relationship into something serious—into marriage—she'd be terrified. She'd sworn in those black days after her husband died that she would never let herself open for that kind of hurt again.

Audra knew with an instant's clarity that the only solution at this time was to get away from Grant and put those feelings in perspective. Grant had said he'd go to the motel to pick up his suticase and make a few more phone calls before he checked out. Since she was scheduled to return the day after tomorrow, they'd decided Grant would spend the day with Audra at Devil's Lake and the night in the cabin tent, so he could help her pack for an early start in the morning.

Before she left she would leave him a note. Audra spent the remainder of the night mentally composing the words—it was hard to do, since she was not sure of his feelings for her. Nor of her own. Perhaps it wouldn't really mean that much to him if she left.

Hugging the blanket closer to her, feeling the chill of the early morning seeping through, Audra resolved to take down the tent as soon as he left and be on her way before he returned. She needed to get to the motel in time before he checked out, so she could leave the note with the manager. She couldn't face Grant again before she left.

After that, she didn't have an exact plan laid out but knew that she wouldn't return to her apartment, in case Grant were to follow her. She would go to her parents' home in Michigan.

In the end, it proved easier than she'd expected. Grant had left early, looking somewhat grim, saying he'd be back in three hours or so.

Audra did not waste any time. She wanted to make sure she was out of Devil's Lake in case he returned sooner than expected. Her packing was not as ordered as usual, and she didn't take the time to sweep the tent free of grit, grass, or insects. She decided to give the gold tent a proper cleaning in her parents' large backyard and rolled it quickly with less than accustomed neatness.

Checking one last time to see if any belongings remained, she then made sure the fire was completely extinguished and that the camp was free of garbage. Driving quickly down to the registration office, she advised them she'd be vacating the lot a day earlier.

She stopped by Grant's motel and noticed with relief that the blue Cadillac was still parked in front of his room. She left the note with the manager, who promised to give it to Grant before he checked out. As she got into the car, she wondered what his reaction would be. The note had read:

Grant:

I'm sorry I have to leave like this, but it's for the best. I'm not sure what my feelings are at this point. You've made me take a good look at myself and at my past, but I don't know if I can put it behind me. Jimmy has been, and always will be, a very important part of my life. And although you've told me it might not bother you if I view you as a sex object, it does bother me. I cannot conduct a relationship on the basis of physical attraction only. The last few days have been special, but very painful. Now that you've forced me to review my life—something I'd tried hard to avoid—I have to get away. Because if I don't put the past in proper perspective, it will always infringe, not only on this relationship, but on any others. I hope you understand. And thank you for some wonderful days—and nights.

Audra

The long drive to her parents' house proved both restful and fruitful. By the time she embraced her surprised parents in the comfortable, cozy living room of their Cape Cod-style home, she had thought of the course she would follow.

After securing their promise not to tell anyone of her plans, Audra began making arrangements for her departure. She called Mona to reassure her that everything was all right and that she'd be going out of town for a while—without disclosing her destination.

The preparations for her trip were conducted without any obstacles and took less time than she'd anticipated. Audra could tell her parents did not approve; she'd told them briefly about Grant but had not disclosed all the details. They felt she should marry again, especially her mother, who told Audra that perhaps she should have given Grant a chance, that she should have discussed things with him.

But how could she discuss feelings she was not sure of? Psychologically, she was a mess at the moment, and needed a total break from her surroundings. And so her parents, although not agreeing, realized that this time their daughter was an independent young woman and offered their help unconditionally.

- *12* -

AUDRA PUT AWAY the airline magazine she'd been browsing through and looked out the small window. The approach to Isla Verde had been announced by the petite, bilingual hostess, and now that they had left the cover of pristine cotton candy clouds, Audra glanced down with burgeoning interest.

The small islands punctuating the Caribbean looked like emeralds nestling in turquoise satin. Leaning back with a contented sigh, Audra felt the thrill of anticipation at shortly becoming part of the Puerto Rican project headquartered in San Juan.

Thinking back over the last few hectic days, Audra felt reasonably satisfied. Her parents had been wonderfully supportive, and Dr. Phillips had smoothed out and expedited all the arrangements to have her join the project—including getting an assistant to cover for the last few classes of her abbreviated summer course.

As the plane bumped to a stop, many passengers were hurriedly collecting cases and purses—despite repeated warnings by the steward to wait until the plane came to a complete halt. Audra moved leisurely, for although she looked forward to seeing the island that was to be her home for the next few months, her excitement was tempered by a floating depression. She reasoned that it was natural to miss Grant at first, but she had to pull herself together, and was determined to combat any lowering of spirits while she assessed her situation.

Lifting her carry-on case and purse with one hand, Audra transferred the jacket of her white suit to her left, along with her thin briefcase. When she stepped into the cool, spacious lounge a short while later, she was pleasurably surprised. She'd heard that in Hawaii the visitor was greeted with flowers; in San Juan, tiny cups of delicious tropical juices replaced the lei.

After thanking the man for the refreshing punch with a rusty *"Muchas gracias"* and receiving a charming grin and *"No hay porqué, mi hermosa señorita"* in return, Audra smiled her thanks again for both the cool drink and the generous compliment. Reflecting she'd allowed enough time for her luggage to have arrived, she headed toward the baggage claim area.

Audra hadn't taken more than a few steps when she heard her name being called. Pivoting, she saw a tall man threading his way through the dispersed pockets of people in her direction. She waited, setting her case down and noted with surprise that the other piece of her tan set was being carried by the brown-haired man.

He put down the suitcase also, and after ascertaining she was indeed Audra Blair, extended a brown hand in a forthright manner.

"My name is Thomas Sutton. Dr. Phillips described you well." He smiled, his gray eyes warm and friendly. "Light brown hair, green eyes, and a terrific figure."

Before Audra could insert anything into his combined introduction and compliment, he continued, "I'm the economist on the project and was lucky enough to get delegated to pick you up."

Audra shook hands with him, liking the firm grip, and looked at him in puzzlement.

"I thought I was supposed to go directly to the hotel, and that I'd be contacted there," she contested as he led her out of the lounge with a hand at her elbow.

"Change in plans. We thought we'd let you acclimate for a couple of days, and as this is only Friday, kill two birds with one stone, to coin an old adage. I've been deputized to show you around the island, and we'll incorporate some of the geography you'll find necessary for your part of the project as we sightsee. You'll report for work on Monday."

He hailed a cab as they emerged into the blinding sunlight, and after putting away her luggage, joined her in the back seat of the taxi. Audra was glad it was air-conditioned and told him so.

"You'll find most of the vehicles we use while doing our research are rather dilapidated, to put it mildly," he grinned. "So enjoy while you can."

Audra groaned, thinking of the pleasant low seventies climate she'd left behind, and she heard Tom Sutton chuckle.

"Relax. It's really not that bad. It's usually not as humid as today."

"Mr. Sutton—"

"Tom, please. We don't stand on formality here. All of us involved in the project have become quite close."

"Tom," she amended, thinking that Tom seemed to want to get on friendlier terms. And although she felt an instant rapport with him, she knew it would never amount to more. Shifting in her seat to face him, she said, "I'd like us to get started right away. I know the study is already in progress, and I was very grateful I was allowed to join at this late date. I also understand the work extends into Saturdays and Sundays, so there's no reason—"

Tom interrupted her gently. "There's no reason for you to start right away. It'll be better if you get used to the climate and familiarize yourself with the island, San Juan in particular. We all did when we first got here."

"If you insist," Audra said doubtfully, thinking that she couldn't wait to work for two reasons: first, she was really excited about the project and the data to be collected and correlated, as well as her chance to put into use her college Spanish; and second, she'd had enough of vacations for a while.

She intended to use this time in Puerto Rico to resolve her feelings. The emotions she had put on ice had caught up with her with a vengeance—and she couldn't accomplish her double-edged mission if she was idle. She needed time and work to put a proper light on things. And she wanted to do a good job on the project, for which she was already late, to justify Dr. Phillips' confidence and trust in her.

Pushing away the disturbing thoughts of Grant crowding her mind, she reflected bitterly that he had really done a fine job of making her face up to her feelings and inflaming them once he'd forced them to surface. Shaking her head, she suggested with inner determination, "Couldn't I get to know the island slowly, on my days off from work?"

"A glutton for punishment, aren't you?" Tom grinned. "You'll find out soon enough days off are scarce. So enjoy this opportunity." Obviously to forestall further argument, he pointed to the disorderly rows of coconut trees.

"They're lovely," Audra said. "Do you know where they originate?"

"I'm afraid not," answered Tom. "Because they grow so profusely in tropical areas, nobody can be sure where they first originated. Among general tree species it reigns supreme."

"That's quite an impressive record for such an unimpressive looking tree," Audra smiled.

"Please don't knock it down, especially around our resident botanist, a native Puerto Rican," warned Tom. "Esteban Rojas waxes poetic on the subject, telling us about its many good qualities, which I'll enumerate."

And he did. For the next few minutes, Tom told her about the many uses—besides the obvious ones of food and drink—of the coconut tree; the tree provided fiber for rope and rugs, the shell was used as a beverage container, the wood was utilized for posts and walking sticks and sometimes for shelter . . .

"Okay, okay, you've convinced me!" laughed Audra.

"Forewarned is forearmed," Tom told her, grinning. "Esteban is a real nice guy, but his overriding passion is the flora of this place—which is a virtual paradise for him."

"They do have a certain . . . elegance," Audra admitted, studying the rows of slender columns until they began to blend into one unending line, when the driver indulged in heart-stopping acceleration as soon as he had an open stretch of road.

After a few minutes the traffic thickened again, and Audra breathed with relief as they traveled at a lower speed. Tom did not seem to see anything amiss, and Audra reflected ruefully that this was probably one of those many things she'd get used to."

Noticing that although the trunks were spaced far apart the rows were unruly, she commented on it, and asked Tom how tall the coconut trees grew.

"They reach a height of one hundred feet. Their growth is not symmetrical enough to be used for guarding wide avenues; the strong ocean winds oftentimes sculpt them into irregular shapes."

As they passed a bright orange stand by the side of the road, Tom told the driver to stop, and Audra was introduced to a *coco frío*—a coconut into which a hole had been cut and a unique straw inserted.

"Delicious, Tom," she finally said, ensconced once more in the cool interior of the car and having finished almost half the contents.

"You looked somewhat peaked," he said, giving her a probing look. "And it seems that anyone who interrupts final work on her thesis and joins a project already begun must have a darn good reason to do so."

Audra met his eyes with directness and told him, "And I hope you're not going to ask me what that reason is."

"No, not at the moment," conceded Tom. "Although I hope you'll let me be your friend and trust me enough to confide in me later on."

"I could really use a friend, Tom, but that is *all* I could be. I have to resolve something," she said softly but firmly.

Tom nodded his understanding, and Audra finished her cold drink with relish. The hot, humid weather was sapping her strength.

The driver stopped again so Tom could dispose of the

two empty shells, and Audra relaxed against the seat, feeling the sleepless nights and the trip and heat catch up with her.

"You'll get used to it soon," Tom told her as she put a hand to her perspiring brow. "The average temp is in the upper seventies." Looking out the window again, he said, "We should be at the hotel in about five minutes. How do you like *camarones?*"

"Testing my Spanish? I love shrimp."

"Good! So do I." A stab pierced her as she remembered that Grant was not particularly fond of fish. Damn the man! Couldn't she even converse without his intruding? Realizing she had missed part of what he'd said, Audra apologized and asked Tom to repeat it.

"I was just asking if you'd like to have dinner with me tonight. I know of a great seafood restaurant."

"I'd love to, but are you sure you can spare the time?"

As the driver entered the long winding drive to the hotel, Tom answered, "I've brought some papers to look over, and I have to make a few phone calls, the first one to Dr. Phillips, to let him know you've arrived safely. But I'll be through in a couple of hours. Seven o'clock sound all right?"

"Fine. I'll meet you in the lobby."

Audra looked at her reflection critically, satisfied that the wan look of the day before had been totally erased by nine hours of sleep. Thoughts of Grant had crowded into her mind, and she awoke once during the night, looking for him instinctively. But luckily, she'd been so drained that she had slept quite deeply after that.

She had trimmed her hair before coming over, since it had grown past its manageable length. Now her page boy hairdo curled softly inward, covering her neck and barely brushing her bare shoulders. It still retained the highlights it'd acquired in Devil's Lake, and Audra was sure it would become even more sun-streaked under the hot tropical rays.

The strapless coral sun dress fitted her more loosely than usual, and Audra realized she'd lost weight. Those first few days away from Grant had taken their toll, when she had welcomed and thrown herself frantically into the preparations to keep her mind off him. But she'd slowly recovered her appetite and was able to sleep nights. She was determined to stand on her own two feet emotionally and come to a decision regarding Grant.

Of course, she suddenly thought, Grant could have made a decision of his own already. Her heart contracted painfully at the idea, and a hot wave of nausea washed over her. But she straightened her shoulders and, picking up her white purse, walked to the door. It was almost ten o'clock, and Tom would be waiting for her down in the lobby.

She saw Tom standing by the brass doors of the hotel as soon as she got out of the elevator. He looked trim and attractive in a pair of dark gray slacks and a matching knit shirt.

His handsome, open features brightened as he turned and caught sight of her. He quickly led her outside to a rented brown Mercury and opened the door for her.

"You're certainly a sight for sore eyes today," he said as he settled beside her. "You must have gotten a good night's sleep."

"I did," Audra said as he merged into the main road. "Where are we going today?"

"Out on the island."

"Aren't we on the island already?" Audra asked, perplexed.

"It's a phrase used to distinguish the rest of Puerto Rico from the metropolitan San Juan area," explained Tom. "How would you like to see the rain forest?"

"I'd love to. Is that its real name, rain forest?"

"It's more of a descriptive term, although quite apt. It's the only tropical forest in the U.S. National Forest system, and more than one hundred billion gallons of rain descend each year."

"With such a rainfall, shouldn't we have bought raincoats and umbrellas?" asked Audra, half seriously.

"Not really. The showers are of a short duration, and there are plenty refuges provided in the picnic areas. Incidentally, the whole forest is a bird sanctuary."

"That certainly shows sound conservation practice," admired Audra.

"Puerto Ricans are very proud of the natural wonders of their island. Not long ago, in nineteen seventy, as a matter of fact, companies with federal authority to export petroleum products were required to contribute to a fund. The Trust Fund in a nonprofit organization which seeks to preserve beautiful areas, as well as those with ecological importance or those that might serve for scientific study."

"Have they been successful?" Audra asked with intense interest.

"More often than not," replied Tom. "One very delicate project was safeguarding the Phosphorescent Bay."

"What was the danger involved?" Audra asked as she settled down more comfortably on the seat.

"Pollution, in the form of overcrowding. The dinoflagellata—miniscule forms of marine life emitting sparks of light when agitated—are present en masse on the south coast."

"What happened?"

"A slight disturbance in the conditions of the bay—a negative environmental change—caused them to lose their brilliance."

Audra was silent for a moment, her thoughts on a subject that was of great importance to her. Then she said quietly, "I've always been interested in ecology—I'm active in a local organization back home, although I haven't been able to contribute much lately—but many times I fear we may be too late to prevent destruction."

"I agree," Tom said, giving her a frankly admiring glance that made Audra feel slightly uncomfortable. Tom seemed a very nice young man; she hoped he didn't get any serious ideas about her. She was still torn about Grant, and didn't want anyone else to go through such pain and uncertainty—especially when she could never reciprocate.

Audra said with false brightness, "Let's not spoil our day with heavy discussions. You didn't tell me anything about the other members of the project over dinner—which, by the way, I'd like to thank you again for. It was the best shrimp I've tasted in a long time." Tom acknowledged her thanks with a smile, and Audra asked, "Approximately how many of us are there?"

"About sixteen or seventeen. I haven't met all of them yet, because some of us went on our separate ways soon after arrival. Dr. Phillips coordinates all activities and is our central point of contact. The majority are social scientists, but we've been lucky to get a couple of secretaries and computer specialists. Dr. Phillips told me last night that we'll be having a get-together in a couple of weeks, so we can all meet those members who are working on separate ends of the island." Tom passed a cart pulled by a donkey and added, "You'll also be expected to attend some social functions given and attended by local dignitaries."

Audra assimilated this piece of information, which called for an immediate revamping of her wardrobe. Turning in the seat, she asked Tom, "Do we have a computer here?"

"Our funding doesn't stretch to that extent." Tom smiled. "We'll be renting some facilities here, as well as feeding data into a central complex in the states."

Tom began reducing speed and announced, "This is it."

Within a few minutes, Tom parked and went around to open Audra's door. As they began walking uphill, Tom told her that over two hundred tree species grew in the area—all native.

Certain sections were dark, because the vegetation was cut off from direct sunlight. Sierra palms and tree ferns intertwined high above. In other parts of the forest, the greenery weaved up and down, allowing clear access to views beyond. The rolling hills in the background appeared a darker shade of green and contrasted brightly with the light gray of the sky and the bright jade of the foliage close by.

Tom directed Audra to a fenced-off waterfall. Once again she was stunned by the symphony of color. The crystalline downward streams seemed to sparkle against the dark gray stones in their sheer descent and were encompassed by luxuriant emerald growth.

"Beautiful, isn't it?" Tom asked her.

"Gorgeous," breathed Audra. "Do a lot of flowers flourish here?"

"Some do. Bromeliads, white ginger, spray of orchids."

"Orchids! I'd love to see some growing in the wild."

"These are hard to find, smaller than the cultivated ones you're used to," Tom told her.

After another few minutes they began walking back, and it took them a half hour to reach the parking lot. Audra turned for one last look before sliding gracefully into the car.

On the way to the Indian Ceremonial Ball Park, which Audra chose over the other attractions Tom suggested, he told her about the Arecibo Observatory, the largest radar-radio telescope in the world, open to the public only on Sundays. He explained that the natural sinkhole in Puerto Rico's karst area reduced excavation costs immensely—it was over three hundred feet deep and was one of the main reasons for situating the observatory there.

Audra enjoyed the visit to the Ball Park and learning about the Tainos, the peaceful group who had carved large stones with inscriptions and figures of gods and who had used the park for religious ceremonies. Since it was still early, they stopped at a small restaurant for dinner and then Tom saw her to her door, telling her he'd help her get settled in the complex the following morning.

Audra glanced at her watch and groaned. She'd be late for the gala event this evening. She had wanted to finish checking out the printouts on population figures and settlement patterns, but a bug in one of the two computers had interpolated some of the data and it had taken longer than she'd planned.

She settled on a quick shower instead of the hot bath she'd been looking forward to and reflected wearily that she had almost caught up with her colleagues during the past three weeks.

Having joined the project later than the rest of them, she'd found herself working from eight to eight, rather than the eight to six the other members put in, needing to cram a tremendous amount of background information into her program. She usually devoted a couple of hours a day in data processing and adjusted the programming as it became necessary.

Her proficiency in Spanish had grown. While a lot of Puerto Ricans in the metropolitan area spoke excellent English, Audra found her knowledge of Spanish was an added plus when gathering field data.

Esteban Rojas and the official interpreter of the team, Ramon Cuencas, had been instrumental in her becoming fluent in so short a time. They spoke to her in Spanish whenever possible and clarified some of the terminology unique to Puerto Rico, such as the word *omnibus,* which here became *guagua,* or the verb *to park,* which she had learned as *estacionar* but which Puerto Ricans had modified from the English and changed to *aparcar.* It was a great asset for Audra to know the language, since she was able to get closer to a lot of people, and make many good friends among those who only spoke Spanish—something which would have been otherwise impossible.

Audra felt a deep sense of satisfaction as she finished dressing. She knew things would become easier in another week and that she'd be able to concentrate more on the program once the preliminary data was collected and inputed. She also knew she'd been doing a good job and had in the process learned a lot.

As she left the complex and drove to the hotel where Dr. Phillips and the rest of the members were probably already congregated, Audra reflected that the time she was spending was not wasted at all. It had been the right decision to take—whatever her motivation at the time— and even though it had meant postponing her thesis, she had already acquired some very valuable practical experience and would acquire a lot more during the next two months.

But although everything with the project was working according to plan, her personal life had not fared as well as her professional one. This time burying herself in her career did not have the same therapeutic effect. She still missed Grant—and it had not lessened as time went on. Though she concentrated at work and did a good job through sheer will power, memories of Grant intruded when least expected. And she had not anticipated she'd be constantly trying to visualize what Grant would be doing—and with whom.

Arriving a half hour late, she noticed most of the contingent was already there, but Dr. Phillips was nowhere to be seen. Audra circulated among the guests, and Tom introduced her to some members she'd not met yet and several Puerto Rican scientists and goverment functionaries.

Excusing herself after an hour of constant introductions and pleasantries, she went to the upstairs ladies' room to freshen up. She found the luxurious black and gold room a haven after all the noise and smoke of the main lounge and rested for a few minutes on a velvet armchair, engaging in a lively conversation with the wife of one of the officials.

Excusing herself from the lovely brunette, Mrs. Rivas, who told her she was going to wait a few more minutes before leaving the peaceful sanctuary, Audra decided she'd been away long enough.

She descended the marble steps of the spiral staircase very carefully on her newly acquired thinly strapped three-inch heels. The cotton dress felt smooth against her skin, and the style, baring one shoulder, flattered her figure and had elicited a fair number of compliments. Upon seeing the classic hostess toga in the softened shade of wild grape in the boutique on Avenida Ashford, she'd known it was the perfect choice.

Despite the last minute rushing, her hairdo had turned out perfect. The cluster of ringlets on top of her head and the two short curls whispering against her cheeks complemented the Roman outline of her gown.

About two-thirds of the way down the stairs Audra stopped to see if she could distinguish Dr. Phillips's snowy head in the crowd milling about the lobby. But he wasn't in view.

She gave another cursory glance at the crowd, her hand lightly resting on the cool balustrade and she was about to continue her descent when her hand tightened convulsively around the marble.

Her eyes picked out a lustrous black head and wide shoulders which towered above the crowd. Her mind tried to erase the image, but her heart began beating rapidly in defiance. Audra stood frozen for a full minute—and then the head of wavy raven hair turned in her direction.

- *13* -

HER EYES LOCKED with steel blue-green, as Grant also stood immobile for a timeless moment. Then he lowered his eyes, releasing her from their mesmerizing effect, and took in her elegant appearance and the pallid texture of her skin, before he made his way purposefully through the thick wall of people and ascended the stairs two at a time.

He stopped two steps below her, which brought him level with Audra. She still gripped the handrail in desperation, as if it were the only solid thing in existence. Everything was spinning around, and even the steps appeared to rise to meet her. Audra put out her hand automatically as if to ward off the fall, and Grant enveloped it in his, squeezing it reassuringly.

"How are you, Audra? You look more beautiful than ever, although you've lost some weight." The normality of his tone and mundaneness of the words brought some

semblance of order into her chaotic world. Her lips curv
in a faint smile at the qualification of his complime
how typical of Grant to casually drop the truth in wheth
palatable or unpalatable.

She removed her hand from his and raised it se
consciously to her neck, encountering the twisted tri
strand of coral and dyed mother-of-pearl supporting t
dramatic shell.

"Lovely choker," Grant said, following her mov
ment, his eyes drawn to the vivid gem of the ocean.

"Thank you." Audra recovered her voice at last,
though she sounded hoarse.

She knew with scary certainty that she was not capab
of facing him at the moment. She had envisioned the
meeting as one further in the future and of her ov
choosing, when her mind would be clear and she h
reached a decision. But now—now she felt the sam
fearful confusion she'd felt when she'd left Devil's Lak
She had not expected his sudden appearance—and it le
her dazed.

So she said coolly, trying to hide her uneasiness, "
you'll excuse me, I have to return to the reception."

Grant's eyes narrowed at her distant tone, and he sa
in a voice laced with irony. "I'm sure Jarvis Phillips ca
spare you for a few moments. The speeches don't co
mence till nine."

"You know Dr. Phillips?" Audra asked in surpris
her heart beating a rapid tattoo.

"I can answer that, and any other questions you ma
have after you answer some of mine," Grant told h
curtly. He took hold of her arm to lead her downstai
and said with veiled command, "Let's go."

Audra did not move except to try and pull away. Gra

didn't release her, but gave her a heart-stopping smile, moved up another step, and put his other arm on her waist. The firm and confident touch scorched through the soft material, and his potent male scent played havoc with her senses. A yearning that was like a physical throe pierced through her, nearly melting her resolve.

"Please, Audra," he said wearily, and she had to fight the impulse to give in. "I just got in and would like nothing better than to relax with a good stiff drink . . . and you." His persuasive tone and the timbre of his voice were a sensual soothing to her tautened nerves.

Realizing that her physical needs were paramount at the moment, Audra clamped down the rush of longing with a desperate effort of will. When she dealt with Grant, she didn't want desire to cloud her thinking.

"I notice in which order I come," she told Grant with deliberate scorn, finally able to enunciate clearly after a charged pause during which she feared her shabby defenses would crumble. Putting all her weight into a sharp tug, Audra managed to elude Grant and ran numbly down the stairs. Although used to low, sensible heels lately during her treks into the hilly countryside, panic imbued her now with instant balance.

Darting one quick look over her shoulder, she saw Grant following her, then seeming to think it over, shrug the broad, dark-jacketed shoulders and halt his pursuit. A wave of relief washed over her, and then all thoughts of Grant were momentarily blacked out when her chairman—a tall, distinguished man in his fifties—found her and began issuing crisp, clear instructions.

The evening passed in a blur. Their findings and suggestions were met with almost full approval, and the representatives of the funding committee were satisfied upon learning that the first part of the study would be completed well within the projected deadline.

After the speeches and reports, many of the people involved with the project and those attending the function removed to the Red Velvet Room for dancing and drinks.

Dr. Phillips proved an excellent dancer when he partnered her for tangos and waltzes, and Tom gave a good account of himself with the ballads. Shortly after midnight, after dancing continuously with numerous partners and finding her facial muscles aching from the forced gaiety she'd assumed for the affair, Audra made her excuses to Dr. Phillips.

She collected the silky shawl shot with silver threads from the cloak room and made her way outside. A figure detached itself from the shadows and stepped into the beam of light escaping the front doors, casting eerie illumination on the silver-blue slag-iron bricks brought over as ballast by Spanish galleons.

Audra faltered on the pavement, her high thin heel embedding itself between two bricks, and Grant's arm shot out to support her.

"Your room or mine?" he asked without preamble.

Audra registered on one plane of her mind, which was seething with anger and confusion, that Grant had changed from his business suit and now wore a hand-woven earth raw-silk jacket, cream cotton broadcloth shirt, linen trousers in a light shade, and a striped silk tie in copper and cream.

"I just showered and changed and had a leisurely dinner," he offered by way of explanation, and added uncompromisingly, "It's high time we talked."

Audra knew Grant would persist, all night if necessary. Rather than argue on the street, she walked over to her dark-blue rented car, and got in the passenger side, tersely giving him directions to the complex.

Grant drove with his usual economy of movement, and within a few minutes they were at her apartment. She opened the door with jerky coordination and stepped inside, allowing Grant to close it.

Without giving him a chance to speak, she faced him defiantly and asked the question uppermost in her mind. "How did you find me?"

"Your parents."

"My parents!" Audra couldn't believe she was hearing right. "You must be a silver-tongued devil," she accused.

A brief, hard smile slashed across Grant's granite features, and he asked, "Would you mind if I sat down?"

Audra put the shawl she was still clutching in clenched fists on the scratched coffee table and, throwing off her silver sandals, settled on a creaky chair, curling her feet under her. She ungraciously motioned for Grant to sit down and noted how his suit clashed with the wild flow-ered print of the couch.

"This is not the order of questions I had in mind, but I'll be generous and set your mind at rest." Audra snorted and the glimmer of a smile lightened the dark blue eyes.

"First of all, let me point out that the reason you saw me so often around campus is that I was more directly involved with the restoration and renovation of the library than you thought—my father's firm is a construction company. I also got to know several faculty members, among them Jarvis Phillips." He loosened his tie and took off his jacket, draping it over the back of the couch. Audra forced herself to keep her eyes on his face and to ignore his movements. "I hadn't connected you with Jarvis when we met. But when I went to visit your parents—Mona gave me that much information—your mother mentioned in passing about how you had been recommended by the chairman of your department for some innovative programming in the social sciences."

Audra groaned and closed her eyes. That was so like her mother—and quite clever, too. She opened her eyes to see Grant regarding her with sympathetic amusement. He continued quietly, "So you can't really blame anyone for giving you away. I was quite certain Mona had guessed where you'd gone, but she was not going to tell me. The only concession I could get from her was your parents' address. I suppose she figured it was up to them to decide whether to tell me or not." He raked his black hair with a tanned hand, and if Audra hadn't known better, she'd have thought he was nervous. "And they wouldn't, either. Your mother's mentioning Jarvis Phillips in passing made everything click into place. I recalled that Jarvis was going to be working during the summer on an important project in Puerto Rico."

His eyes seemed to understand her conflicting emotions because he asked harshly, "Are you now regretting the days we spent together?" He rose and came to stand next to her, overpowering her with his potent masculine presence and the rawness of his anger. "It seemed to me you had no reservations at the time."

Audra stood up also and clasped her cold hands together. Wanting to buy some time, she asked, "Would you like something to drink? I only keep brandy, so there's not much of a selection." She tried to keep her voice steady, but her inner turmoil overflowed into her speech.

"What are you having?" Grant asked, opening the top

buttons of his shirt. Her eyes were drawn irresistibly to the light covering of black curly hair, and with aching effort she glanced away and turned toward the kitchen.

"Coffee. Is that all right?" she asked over her shoulder. Grant's voice made her jump, rippling directly behind her.

"Fine." His calm answer unruffled her composure even further.

Audra moved around the confining space, experiencing a panicky suffocation at the way his lean body seemed to fill the room. The masculine scent of him, his lemon-lime lotion, contributed to making her nerves raw.

Her hand trembled as she went about the familiar task of preparing coffee, but she managed not to drop anything. Grant kept silent vigil, and Audra felt like screaming at him to go away.

The coffee finally ready, she got cups, saucers, napkins, sugar, milk, and coffee pot arranged on a lacquered tray. Grant moved to one side, but took the shaky tray from her and indicated for Audra to precede him. Setting the tray on the round table in front of the love seat, he poured for Audra and himself. She was secretly thankful for his doing the honors but didn't verbalize it beyond a curt, "Thanks."

"Why couldn't we talk about it, Audra?" The quiet question, although she had been expecting it, startled her, and she scalded her upper lip on the hot, black liquid.

After all this time, Audra was afraid to give him an answer. She knew as soon as she'd seen him that the chemistry was still there. She was in fact right now fighting the urge to ask him to take her to bed. But that had been the problem from the beginning; Grant had overpowered her and Audra didn't like the helpless feeling. She wanted to think she had some control over her life, but since meeting Grant, her carefully reconstructed world had been in a state of constant upheaval.

Taking a sip of the steaming liquid, she put the cup down on her lap and looked at it for a long moment, as if it held life's answers. Then, with a deep sigh, she decided that Grant deserved the truth; he'd always been upfront with her.

Meeting the opalescent gaze, Audra said softly, "I am not ashamed of those days we spent together. The reason I left is that I was still scared. I didn't know where we were heading, and I didn't like the power you held over me."

"And you like everything guaranteed, don't you, Audra?" Grant said scathingly. "After the death of your husband and the collapse of your safe little world, you hid behind work. And while your interests have made you the vital person you are, they have also shielded you from reality."

Audra recognized the truth in what he'd said, but there was more to it, and she told him so. "It's far more complex than that." She put down her cup on the end table and laced her fingers together to still their trembling. Looking at him directly, she told him in a low but firm voice, "I want you, Grant. I want you so badly that I have to keep myself from going over to the couch and making love to you." A strange light entered his eyes, but Audra ignored it. "And that was one of the main reasons I left. I knew you'd be able to stop me—and I don't mean by force," she added with a tinge of bitterness to her smile, "and I had to get away and confront my feelings without outside stimuli." This time her smile was genuine as she added, "And the kind of stimuli you provide are too powerful to ignore and quite hard to resist."

Grant walked over to where she sat and pulled her up, keeping one hand loosely about her waist. "Are you saying that if I were to start making love to you now you wouldn't be able to resist or stop yourself?"

Audra felt her heart beating against her agitated breast like a wild bird seeking escape. Her mouth was dry as she answered him, "Anything is possible," she said, licking her lips, "but I'd say the odds are with you."

Grant lowered his head slowly and tasted her lips with controlled mastery. Audra didn't attempt to return the kiss, concentrating on keeping a hold on her emotions. His lips feathered a trail from her mouth to her nose and back down to her chin. Then he returned to her lips and he concentrated on each corner of her mouth, nibbling gently on the curves. Audra felt the small flame growing, and it was suddenly fanned into full blaze as he boldly sought admission with the tip of a velvety tongue. Audra tasted the sweet coffee on the invading flesh and moaned when his tongue engaged hers in an age-old battle.

Then his mouth was leaving hers and descended to her throat, settling first on the pulse beating madly in tandem with the blood racing scaldingly through her veins, and then on the sensitive cord of her neck, sharply biting and sucking the sensitive flesh, before returning once more to claim complete and burning possession of her mouth.

When he lifted his mouth from hers after a golden moment in time, Audra knew that if he picked her up and carried her into her bedroom, she'd offer no objections. In fact, as the sensual haze enveloped her, she was hoping he would.

But Grant walked away from her and rubbed his neck in a tired motion, and Audra belatedly realized he had not even held her in his arms. His lovemaking had been fleeting and still Audra felt shaken from the mind-shattering experience.

He finally turned around to face her, and Audra saw on his tense features the effort it had cost him to pull away. He told her quietly, "You have really matured in many ways, Audra. And I won't take advantage of the trust you placed in me when you told me you wanted me. You might be carried on a tide of passion now, but you'd hate yourself—and especially me—in the morning. And my relationship with you means a hell of a lot more than instant gratification."

"What *does* our relationship mean to you, then?" Audra asked. "It can't have been that important if you took so long to follow me." Audra realized she was not being entirely rational, but her feelings were placing urgent demands on her and she wanted answers.

"Besides having to find out where you were, I also had to make arrangements at work to take some time off. The crisis that arose while we were at Devil's Lake had vital ramifications, and I had to spend two weeks in Europe to settle it entirely. As soon as I was able to come here, I did."

He picked up his jacket and tie and said in a firm tone, "But I have to have an answer. So far, I've done all the chasing. I've followed you here, which should demonstrate that you mean more than a one-night stand— if you ever could have been so foolish as to doubt it.

But the next move has to come from you."

Audra felt the rush of panic hit her which she'd felt every time she dug deep into her feelings to make a decision about Grant. He'd been right when he said she buried herself in her work to avoid facing up to her own emotions.

"I've told you before that the physical aspect of our relationship is perfect, but there has to be more," Audra said with desperation threading her voice. "Our relationship has to be based on more than considering each other as sex objects."

"That's not how I view you," Grant countered calmly, but she saw a shadow pass over the gleaming dark-blue eyes when he said, "And if your viewing me as a sex object doesn't bother me, I don't see why it should worry you."

"But I haven't resolved my own feelings," Audra insisted, feeling a helpless sense of frustration at his own certainty.

"It's time you did," Grant said as he walked toward the door.

"Just don't rush me," Audra told him. "I'd like us to spend some time together—but without going to bed."

Grant's eyes narrowed into glittery slits and a muscle worked in his jaw. "That might not be possible over an extended period of time."

"Over the next few days," Audra said hopefully. "We could go to public places, get to know one another."

"I know all I need to know about you," he said then relented. "All right. I'll try to give you room this time and not 'overpower' you, as you've put it." As he opened the door, he said in grim warning, "But you have to realize that it works both ways—you have an effect on me I have no wish to control, and I certainly didn't come here to conduct a platonic relationship." His last words hung in the air long after he'd closed the door behind him: "You'll have to make up your mind. One way or the other. And soon."

- 14 -

WHEN THEY ARRIVED at El Morro from San Cristóbal, the sun was casting its most potent rays and the heat enveloped everything in a shimmering haze. The sky was an immaculate blue, with no cloud to mar its uniform perfection, and the aquamarine waters beat against the fortification in a timeless struggle. The fortress, rising one hundred forty feet above the Atlantic, a mammoth composed of six levels and labyrinthine tunnels, offered a magnificent view from its ramparts. The old black cannons were silent sentinels staring perpetually out to sea.

Grant had told her he'd visited the fortress a few years back on a business trip, but he'd gone along with Audra's wish to see it a third time. She loved old buildings, especially castles, and had confided to Grant that two of the places she'd always wanted to visit were Germany and Austria.

Audra walked toward the thick surrounding wall, the forceful winds playing with her split-skirt sun dress, its airy, gauze peasant style refreshing in the heat. Her hair was put up in a ponytail, the red band holding it up the same vivid shade of her outfit.

"You really like old things, don't you?" Grant said as he came to stand next to her, leaning against the ancient stone.

Audra looked at him intently, to gauge whether criticism was implied. But she read none in the blue-green eyes which matched the color of the ocean in the distance.

"I do. The first time I came here it was sort of rushed, with some of the members of the project. The second time it was with a guide tour, like that one over there," she pointed to a young man dressed in black pants and a red jacket, apparently oblivious to the burning rays of the sun, who was directing his group near to the spot where Audra and Grant stood. "While it was quite instructive, I found that I missed some of what my tour guide was saying, so I bought a couple of brochures and magazines and read up on it."

The young man, obviously bilingual, was telling his group, "San Juan's role as a strong point began about fifteen thirty-three with the building of the Fortaleza. An impressive but by no means impregnable structure, it served as a bastion, treasure storehouse, and then as residence of Puerto Rico's governors. After almost five hundred years, it still performs the last function."

"It must have been quite an undertaking," Grant said, referring to the building of the Fortaleza. As he shifted position, his muscles rippled under the black-and-white print silk shirt tightly encasing his powerful torso.

"And a hurried one, too," Audra said, dragging her

eyes away from his compelling masculinity. "With the Elizabethan era, the English replaced the French as the menace, and the Council of the Indies recognized the need for a Caribbean defense plan."

"When was it completed?" Grant's gaze skimmed lightly over her face, and she resented his cool impassiveness.

"Construction began in fifteen eighty-six on the powerful fortress of El Morro. Menendez, then governor of the Indies, reported to the council with confidence that the fort would be 'the strongest that his Majesty hath in all the Indies.'"

"Did his statement prove true?"

"Many times." Audra nodded, leaning her elbows on the lower part of the undulating formation, as she warmed to her subject. "El Morro was finished in the nick of time. In fifteen ninety-five, November, if I recall accurately, as the flagship of a heavily laden Spanish treasure fleet lay disabled in San Juan harbor, down swooped a force led by Sir Francis Drake. He was counting on surprise as an ally, but the gunners of El Morro were ready for him and their aim was excellent. He was really lucky during the campaign, because a shot went crushing through the walls of the cabin, missing him by a hair and killing two of his companions."

"It must have been ego-deflating for a man of his stature," Grant commented with male empathy.

"I imagine so. According to Puerto Rican history, he fought and maneuvered for three days, but finally had to retreat or lose his fleet." Audra's voice was soft as she visualized the battle in her mind.

"I think I can understand his frustrations quite well," Grant said in a tone which tinted her cheeks pink.

Ignoring his comment, Audra continued, "Drake covered his chagrin with the boast that he would lead his men to 'twenty places' far more wealthy and easier to be gotten."

As he began walking again, Grant asked, "Were the defenses ever breached?"

Audra trailed him slowly, feeling her pulse leap erratically at the sight of the tall figure strolling with animal grace. His long legs, covering the ground effortlessly with pantherlike movements, reminded her of Devil's Lake and his powerful lovemaking.

"Tired, or bored of the company?" he asked when he realized she was not following him, one eyebrow flickering upward as he eyed her coolly.

"Neither," Audra denied, moving at a slight tangent to battle the desire that seemed just below the surface ever since he'd come back into her life only the day before.

Turning at an angle from him, she showed him an outwardly tranquil profile. Inside, she was a mass of quivering nerves. The salty ocean breeze ruffled her pony tail, and she noticed out of her peripheral vision that it had boyishly tousled the black, wavy hair. As she smoothed the grainy texture of the balwark with her palms, she felt its coolness restore some of her composure.

"In answer to your question," she continued quietly, "the defenders of San Juan found out that not every adversary would be defeated. In fifteen ninety-eight, the Earl of Cumberland employed an unexpected strategy in trying to secure Puerto Rico for Queen Elizabeth."

Grant came over to join her, and her gaze ricocheted from his blue-green brilliance. She supported her body on her outstretched palms, bracing them against the ramparts.

"Cumberland avoided the harbor of San Juan and landed his troops on a deserted beach east of the town. An epidemic had been raging through the town, and the garrison was weak and outnumbered. The imminence of starvation forced them to surrender after a fortnight."

"What about Cumberland and his men? Were they victims of the epidemic too?" Grant asked with interest, becoming caught up in the gripping tale.

"That's why he could not consolidate his victory," Audra replied, smiling at the sharpness of Grant's observation. "The plague raged among his own troops, and he was forced to give up his dream of keeping the island for England. He loaded his ships with all the hides, ginger, and sugar he could find and set sail."

"He can't have been recieved too well back home," Grant said wryly.

"You're right. He was severely critized for bringing such a poor booty and losing several hundred men."

Grant looked at her, an undecipherable light in his eyes. "You seem to have gained a lot of knowledge in a very short time." Audra shrugged her shoulders, and looked at the distance, where blue sky met blue-green water. "It's too bad that you don't concentrate half as much energy in dealing with the present."

It was the first time he'd referred to their discussion of last night, and Audra lifted worried eyes at his harsh tone. She had been happy about her temporary reprieve but was afraid, with sinking certainty, that Grant was about to end it.

"Grant," she began, wanting to stop him from saying

what she was sure was coming, but he walked on again, and Audra followed reluctantly. He finally stopped in a narrow passage between high walls, at the end of which a domed stone structure could be glimpsed.

"Let's go over there," he suggested, clasping Audra's hand and leading her in the direction he'd indicated.

Then he motioned for her to precede him, and because of his broad shoulders, he had to advance down the tubular hall sideways. Audra came to the end and began to turn back.

"There's no exit," she announced. "We have to—"

The rest of the sentence remained unsaid as Grant flung out an arm and pulled her toward him. His hands slid slowly down below her waist, drawing her even closer, the heat of his body intensified by the rays beating down on them, the blood rushing in her ears blending with the susurrant sound of the ocean.

One hand stayed on her hip, molding her to him and making her aware of his totally male arousal, and the other cupped her neck, bringing her face inexorably closer to his. He ravaged the softness of her trembling lips, devouring her strength by degrees. As her initial resistance ebbed, the bruising pressure of his mouth declined. When she began to respond with impassioned ardency he eased back.

"I have to know something. Are you in love with that boy I saw you dancing with last night?"

Audra knew Grant could only mean Tom—although he hardly qualified for the term as he was twenty-eight. Deeming it wise not to correct Grant at the moment, she shook her head, strands of hair bouncing against her neck at her vehemence. "No, I'm not. He's been one of th most supportive persons in the project, and I consider him a good friend."

"Are you sleeping with him?" Grant's tone was grating, and Audra moved uneasily in his bone-breaking embrace.

Audra looked at him and asked softly, "Wouldn't you know if I had?"

He exhaled his breath in a sharp motion and told her roughly, "Yes. I'd know."

Gripping her chin, he told her, studying her expression intently, "He's in love with you."

"Tom?" she said, but was not really surprised. She'd been aware from the beginning that Tom had wanted her as more than a friend, and had been afraid it would happen. Recalling certain incidents, she was sure Grant was right and her heart went out to Tom. They still had to work together for a few weeks.

"I arranged to have a week off from work," Grant said, "but I won't be staying that long." Audra paled, the very thing she'd feared most coming to pass. "You've had four years to recover from your husband's death and over a month to think about our relationship." She felt pain and dread, but he continued relentlessly. "I'll give you one more night. I don't intend to wait any longer for a decision that you're too afraid to make. It would be self-defeating for both of us." Releasing her chin and moving away from her, he said with finality. "You know where to find me. If I don't hear from you tomorrow, I'll be taking the evening flight and will consider that your answer."

Audra watched him walk away through the blur of unshed tears. Leaning against the cold, sandpaper-rough stone, she felt even worse than when she'd received the news of Jimmy's death.

She never knew how she made it back to her apartment, but once inside the familiar surroundings, some of her thinking processes were restored. She made some tea and toast, not feeling the least bit of appetite but knowing she should have something.

The evening was interminable, the minutes and hours blending into each other with hopeless slowness. When she went to bed, she felt a terrifying loneliness eating at her insides, and the knowledge that she was solely responsible did not help matters, or help vanquish her empty, overriding bitterness.

In the long hours of the night, Audra realized what she'd been avoiding all along: she was in love with Grant. Although she liked Tom, found him interesting and attractive, she'd been able to tell Grant without a shadow of a doubt that she was not in love with him.

Her failure to admit the truth stemmed from her protective self-deception. Audra had been so used to withdrawing from any relationships that could turn serious that it had become second nature. She had been falling for Grant all along—ever since that unorthodox meeting in the library, where her fear had not been unfounded. Grant had proved her right—he had constituted a real threat because, besides overpowering her senses, he'd taken her heart.

Audra had deluded herself into thinking that the attraction was based only on sex. And although their chemistry had proved combustible, Audra saw that she would not have felt so panicky that last night at Devil's Lake if she had not realized—subconsciously, perhaps—that her defenses had been breached.

Her growth process, halted by her fear of getting hurt again—losing someone she loved again—had been completed by Grant. He had refused to force her or seduce her, to take away from her free will and responsibility. He had not played on her body's needs, but instead had forced her to recognize and come to terms with them on her own.

Audra knew she must take that chance. Resisting the urge to run to him in the night, Audra decided to wait until morning. She was through with running and not analyzing her actions.

A new fear gnawed at her as she faced the fact that Grant might not be in love with her. It didn't seem likely that a man of Grant's integrity and self-possession would be chasing the conquest that got away. And yet he'd never actually told her he was in love with her. It was quite possible that Grant could have become tired with her failure to face reality and acknowledge her real feelings.

As the scarlet orb of the sun climbed the gray, dull sky, banishing the shadows from her room, Audra resolved that she would not let fears and uncertainties stop her this time. She loved him, she told herself as she got out of bed to take a long, luxurious bubble bath, and she must trust him. She would go to him on his terms and prove to him she was now the mature, equal partner he deserved.

- *15* -

It was after ten when Audra arrived at Grant's hotel. As she walked through the plush lobby, her white heels sinking in the deep black and white carpeting reflecting the color scheme of the ornate furnishings, Audra felt as if the butterflies in her stomach had formed into an army to launch an attack on its fragile lining.

When she asked for Grant's room number, the clerk told her regretfully that Mr. Williams was out. Panicky, Audra asked the man if he had checked out and felt her heart return to its rightful spot when the clerk quickly assured her that Mr. Williams was out sightseeing.

With sudden clarity, Audra knew where he was. Thanking the man, she clutched her small purse tightly against her taut body and practically ran out of the hotel.

She sighed in frustration when the traffic prevented her from flying to her destination. She smiled ruefully at her own fancy that each minute that passed seemed an hour when it really was no more crowded than usual. After all her procrastination, she now couldn't wait to give Grant her decision. And now it seemed as if an eternity would transpire before she ever reached El Morro.

Audra walked for about ten minutes before she was able to spot Grant. Seeing Grant's broad back straining the sky-blue material, his long, muscular legs bracing him against the yellow-gray parapet, his raven hair buffeted by the strong winds, Audra felt paralyzed. Last minute doubts and anxiety flooded through her. What if she was wrong? What if he didn't love her?

Sensing her presence, Grant turned around. His smoothly chiseled features were impassive, his ocean eyes expressionless. He made no move, but merely looked at her across the intervening distance.

Audra swallowed the lump in her dry, burning throat and nervously licked her lips, seeing his eyes follow the movement of her tongue, as they had many times before. But whereas before his eyes had burned with passion as they concentrated on the curve of her lips, this time his cool blue-green gaze returned swiftly to the uncertainty she knew was in hers.

Needlessly rearranging the pleats of her dress, Audra forced her legs to take one step, then another, until she finally reached his side. Although his eyes burned with that strange light she'd seen before, he still did not speak. The fear and anguish in Audra was suddenly expressed in anger. Grant could make it easier for her, but he stood there like a block of ice.

Rage exploding before her eyes in a multicolored mist, she lashed out at him. "Damn you! How dare you do this to me?" Her voice, at first wavery and raspy, gained rapidly in strength, and within seconds she found she had to contain herself from shouting at him. "I was right about you the first time I ever had the misfortune to lay eyes on you. You're a heartless brute, and I don't know how I could ever have imagined myself in love with you."

Pausing one moment in her tirade to gulp down a torrent of air, she continued in a low, furious tone. "As a matter of fact, the only reason I came here today was to tell you exactly what I thought of you. Don't think for a single minute..."

Her words were cut off abruptly as Grant embraced her in the middle of the fortress, and soon there gathered an amused crowd of spectators who applauded as he silenced her with a breath-stealing kiss.

Grant took a bow for the benefit of the smiling tourists, and Audra, trying to recover from the kiss, which had left her weak but still in fighting form, tried to pull away from his encircling arm in stiff, belated dignity.

"Oh no you don't!" Grant whispered softly in her ear. "You're not getting away this time. I'm tired of chasing you." He reinforced his statement with another possessive kiss, which Audra cut short, embarrassed by the people looking at them.

The drive to Grant's hotel did not seem to take any time at all now, with Audra comfortably ensconced in the seat next to him, his arm draped tightly over her shoulders as if afraid she'd disappear again.

There were no preliminaries as soon as the door closed after them. Audra and Grant undressed each other and they tumbled into bed with burning urgency, her arms rising wordlessly for his possession, his knee nudging her thighs apart as he took her in desperate need.

As they lay still joined, their bodies moist and their

hot, gasping breaths mingling together, Grant murmured, "You sure took your sweet time deciding how you felt about me."

"What about you?" Audra accused, still remembering those awful moments at the Fortaleza.

Understanding her pain, he brushed his lips against her love-swelled ones in an attempt to erase it. "I had to be sure, Audra," he told her with regret threading his voice.

"You must have known that I was in love with you when I sought you out," Audra said, looking up at him, sure the fullness of her love was reflected in her gaze.

Grant nuzzled her neck and answered quietly. "I had to be really sure it was love, not just sex," he said, smiling at the astounded expression in her eyes.

"Then it *did* bother you," she exclaimed, trying to sit up, but finding it impossible with the heavy weight that imprisoned her under its hard warmth. "Talk about double standards," she added, incensed.

Grant's chuckle penetrated her chest, and Audra gasped as both the sound and the rubbing contact began tapping the smoldering nerve endings of her body. Grant noticed her response, and he raised on his elbows to deliberately rub his chest against the hardening fullness of her breasts.

Audra gasped as the mat of hair on his chest brought her nipples into full, throbbing erectness, and she bit his shoulder with sharp playfulness.

"It wouldn't have mattered with another woman. But I fell in love with you that first night in your tent—and it scared the hell out of me that you might not come to love me."

"You knew as long ago as that?" Audra asked, getting quite upset again, but not upset enough to demand that he remove his body from hers. "And it took me so long to finally stop lying to myself. Why didn't you tell me sooner? You certainly could have saved me the hurt and fear of this morning."

Grant rolled onto his back, and Audra moved so that she lay half across his bronzed body. "What would you have done if I had confessed my love for you that night in your cabin tent—or even at the motel?" Audra's silence gave him her answer; she would have run that much sooner. "I also had to make sure that you were still not in love with Jimmy, or something I could fight even less—his memory and the idolizing we sometimes feel toward those who are no longer with us.

"I had to give you time, and I also had to refrain from blurting it out during our lovemaking—which took some doing—so that you wouldn't think it was a facile declaration in the heat of passion."

"One thing is certain," Audra said, playing with the curly hair on his chest. "All ghosts of Jimmy are gone forever."

He dropped a kiss on top of her head, sighing deeply. "You don't know the agony I went through those first few days after you left. I went out of my mind, thinking that something might have happened to you."

"Think of it this way," she said gravely. "Whenever you start taking me for granted, you only have to remember what it felt like losing me."

Grant rolled her onto her back, spread-eagling her, and began to nuzzle her in punishment. "Never say something like that again. Never!" Audra heard the residue of worry and fear in Grant's voice, and she said lightly, "I promise."

Grant was not entirely satisfied, and he started to tickle

her in earnest, until Audra whispered against his neck, "Don't you think my hands might serve a better purpose if you set them free?"

Grant must have thought her idea had a great deal of merit, because he released her hands immediately. Audra pushed him onto his back, and began a trail of kisses on his body, starting with his forehead and continuing down past his neck. When she reached his chest, Audra kissed first one male nipple, then the other, delighting in his sharp inhalation of breath. Her tongue licked the small hardened peaks, and her hands continued the caress as she lowered her mouth to the flat, hard stomach and stabbed at his navel. Grant groaned and pulled her on top of him. He helped her accommodate her body over his.

Audra moaned as she put her hands on either side of Grant to support the weight of her body. His hands traveled the length of her, encouraging her into a smooth, slow rhythm. Grant gently massaged the base of her spine, caressed her rounded buttocks, and then went around to her breasts, cupping the hardened mounds and rolling the nipples between thumb and forefinger until Audra felt like screaming from the intense arousal. Her hips began a quicker motion, and Grant arched upward to meet her, grabbing her waist to make them move as one.

Audra felt herself rising quickly to the top of a volcano, her body beginning to be shaken by the tremors, her blood molten lava coursing through her veins. She lowered her head to kiss Grant, and his tongue searched the recesses of her mouth, caressing teeth and roof, and dueling with hers. As he felt her convulsions begin, he molded her even closer to his body, until Audra felt as one in their concurrent release. She gasped his name over and over again and heard Grant groaning hers, and when she collapsed on top of him, her breath gone, her chest heaving, her body moist with their combined dampness, he turned her over onto her back and took her to the heights again, the aftershocks mingling with the new tremors he induced in her. As Audra reached the summit, she cried, "I love you," and heard his muffled response against her hair as she erupted again in unison with Grant in a conflagration of passion.

As they lay satiated in the quiet aftermath, Audra unconsciously sighed. Grant propped himself on an elbow and looked down at her in concern. "What's wrong, kitten?" The open love and desire evident in the blue-green gaze flooded her with joy and warmth, and Audra raised her head to drop a soft kiss on the sensuous male lips.

"I was just thinking of Tom—" Audra stopped, horrified, and her eyes flew to his to see if Grant was angry at her slip.

The smile curving his lips showed he knew what was running through her mind. "You don't have to worry about mentioning other people when we are in bed. You've told me you're not in love with Tom. He's quite a different proposition from a husband I thought you still loved."

"I did love Jimmy, but I had gotten over his loss before I met you. I guess I just used him as a shield to prevent you from getting too close and to prevent myself from admitting my real feelings."

"I'm glad it didn't work," Grant said, lying down

again and folding her body into the curve of his. "I couldn't take it much longer and therefore had to shock you into a decision."

"You certainly succeeded in shocking me," Audra said wryly.

"What were you thinking about Tom?" he asked her as she began circling motions on his leg with her toe.

"That I'm sorry for him. If he really is in love with me as you said, it's going to be painful for him the next few weeks. I just want him to be as happy as I am now."

"I'm certain he's realized by now that you're not in love with him. When you go back to work, you can tell him you'll be marrying me."

"Is that so?" Audra asked, ready to debate the issue. "I don't recall hearing any proposals."

Grant gave her nose a nip and said, "After possessing you, do you think I'll ever let you go? That's why you shouldn't feel so sorry for Tom. He's had the privilege of knowing you, and he's lucky he can consider himself your friend."

They were silent for a while, both lost in their own thoughts, until Audra brought up the abandoned subject.

"I still have not heard a proposal," she told him, her toe increasing the area of circumference on his flesh.

He surprised Audra by jumping from the bed and extracting a square package from his briefcase. "I've been carrying this since that morning in Wisconsin when I supposedly went out for breakfast. I was going to ask you to marry me the night before we left Devil's Lake."

Audra took the emerald engagement ring out, the color of her tear-bright eyes, and gave it to Grant to put on her finger. "This was certainly a well-guarded secret." Holding it up to the light, she said with a saucy smile,

"I thought you were up to something that day, but I never dreamed it'd be something honorable. And then of course you made me forget about other things that morning."

"I made you?" Grant laughed, his deep chuckle rippling over her skin. "You were a heartless temptress that day."

"As I recall, you certainly got even the following night," Audra said dryly.

"Still mad?" Grant asked, his tongue licking the rounded curve of her shoulder.

"No," Audra shook her head, smiling. "It just gives me ideas for when *you* step out of line."

"Want to start right now?" he asked, pinning her down with his body.

She pushed at his shoulders, but Grant settled down comfortably on top of her, one of his elbows supporting some of his weight so she could breathe comfortably.

"And you called me insatiable." His mouth started coming down on hers, and Audra turned her head, trying to evade the male lips, yelping, "No, please, Grant. We have to talk."

"That's all we've *been* doing," he told her as he switched his sensual attack to the tender curve of her neck.

Audra held his head between her hands so he'd be forced to stop. "We have to make plans, Grant. I still have about two months left here in Puerto Rico."

Grant's expression sobered, and he said after a minute, "It's going to be hard at first. I'll just have to do a lot of weekend commuting for the rest of this summer."

"Will you be able to get away? I wish I could, but we usually work Saturdays or Sundays, sometimes both."

"I'll change my schedule around over the next few

weeks. We'll manage," he told her with a slow, heart-stopping smile, and Audra breathed easier, knowing he'd find a way.

"But," he told her as he pushed back damp strands of hair which had come undone from her short French braid. Audra smiled as he released the bit of gathered hair which still remained on top of her head, since most of it had collapsed as soon as he'd begun making love to her. "But," he repeated, "I don't want to wait until the end of the summer to marry you. When's the first long week-end you'll have?"

"In two weeks. I'm due to take a Monday off, but I'm sure Dr. Phillips won't mind my taking Tuesday off also. I'll work even longer the week before to make sure I'm able to."

"Just be careful that you don't get sick. I don't want you disabled on our wedding night."

"Not even if I'm confined to bed?" Audra asked.

Grant grinned, and said, "I rather appreciate participation in lovemaking. And judging by your recent performance, your participation is increasing at an amazing rate."

"Any objections?" Audra asked, releasing the hard, lean cheeks to put her arms around his neck.

"None at all. What about you? Any objections to getting married in Michigan in two weeks?"

"None at all," Audra teased back. "When I called Mona before I left, she told me her wedding is planned for November and that she wanted me to be in the wedding party. So I'll just ask her to be my maid of honor at our small reception—I'm sure she'll expect it. I should be finished with my thesis by then," she added with a sigh of relief.

"Then we can have our honeymoon in November," Grant said with satisfaction, "away from everything and everyone." Looking down into her eyes, he asked, "Are you sure you won't mind getting married in such a short time, instead of waiting and having a larger reception?"

"I'm sure," Audra smiled. "I don't want to wait any longer either. The important thing is that my parents be able to attend." Shifting her body provocatively beneath his, she asked, "What were you thinking of in terms of our honeymoon?"

"I know you've always wanted to travel, but I thought we might do that down the road a bit. I'd like you to myself for a while and was thinking in terms of a cabin in Alaska, which I've been contemplating buying."

"Sounds marvelous," she reassured him unequivocally, dropping little kisses on the strong column of his neck. "I hear the nights are long there."

"Just as I said the first time I laid eyes on you," Grant grinned, his eyes a smoldering dark blue, "a woman after my own heart."

"I thought you were tired of talking, Mr. Williams. I have only a few more hours before I have to go back to work. Can't you think of more exciting things to do until then?"

Audra saw the opalescent eyes burning with love and desire before she closed her eyes as his mouth claimed hers, and his legs parted her thighs, showing her that indeed he had more exciting things to do until morning.

_____ 06195-6 **SHAMROCK SEASON #35** Jennifer Rose
_____ 06304-5 **HOLD FAST TIL MORNING #36** Beth Brookes
_____ 06282-0 **HEARTLAND #37** Lynn Fairfax
_____ 06408-4 **FROM THIS DAY FORWARD #38** Jolene Adams
_____ 05968-4 **THE WIDOW OF BATH #39** Anne Devon
_____ 06400-9 **CACTUS ROSE #40** Zandra Colt
_____ 06401-7 **PRIMITIVE SPLENDOR #41** Katherine Swinford
_____ 06424-6 **GARDEN OF SILVERY DELIGHTS #42** Sharon Francis
_____ 06521-8 **STRANGE POSSESSION #43** Johanna Phillips
_____ 06326-6 **CRESCENDO #44** Melinda Harris
_____ 05818-1 **INTRIGUING LADY #45** Daphne Woodward
_____ 06547-1 **RUNAWAY LOVE #46** Jasmine Craig
_____ 06423-8 **BITTERSWEET REVENGE #47** Kelly Adams
_____ 06541-2 **STARBURST #48** Tess Ewing
_____ 06540-4 **FROM THE TORRID PAST #49** Ann Cristy
_____ 06544-7 **RECKLESS LONGING #50** Daisy Logan
_____ 05851-3 **LOVE'S MASQUERADE #51** Lillian Marsh
_____ 06148-4 **THE STEELE HEART #52** Jocelyn Day
_____ 06422-X **UNTAMED DESIRE #53** Beth Brookes
_____ 06651-6 **VENUS RISING #54** Michelle Roland
_____ 06595-1 **SWEET VICTORY #55** Jena Hunt
_____ 06575-7 **TOO NEAR THE SUN #56** Aimee Duvall
_____ 05625-1 **MOURNING BRIDE #57** Lucia Curzon
_____ 06411-4 **THE GOLDEN TOUCH #58** Robin James
_____ 06596-X **EMBRACED BY DESTINY #59** Simone Hadary
_____ 06660-5 **TORN ASUNDER #60** Ann Cristy
_____ 06573-0 **MIRAGE #61** Margie Michaels
_____ 06650-8 **ON WINGS OF MAGIC #62** Susanna Collins

All of the above titles are $175 per copy

Available at your local bookstore or return this form to:

SECOND CHANCE AT LOVE
Book Mailing Service, P.O. Box 690, Rockville Cntr., NY 11570

Please send me the titles checked above. I enclose _____
Include 75¢ for postage and handling if one book is ordered; 50¢ per book for
two to five. If six or more are ordered, postage is free. California, Illinois, New
York and Tennessee residents please add sales tax.

NAME _____

ADDRESS _____

CITY_____ STATE/ZIP_____

Allow six weeks for delivery.   **SK-41**

_____ 05816-5 DOUBLE DECEPTION #63 Amanda Troy
_____ 06675-3 APOLLO'S DREAM #64 Claire Evans
_____ 06680-X THE ROGUE'S LADY #69 Anne Devon
_____ 06687-7 FORSAKING ALL OTHERS #76 LaVyrle Spencer
_____ 06689-3 SWEETER THAN WINE #78 Jena Hunt
_____ 06690-7 SAVAGE EDEN #79 Diane Crawford
_____ 06691-5 STORMY REUNION #80 Jasmine Craig
_____ 06692-3 THE WAYWARD WIDOW #81 Anne Mayfield
_____ 06693-1 TARNISHED RAINBOW #82 Jocelyn Day
_____ 06694-X STARLIT SEDUCTION #83 Anne Reed
_____ 06695-8 LOVER IN BLUE #84 Aimée Duvall
_____ 06696-6 THE FAMILIAR TOUCH #85 Lynn Lawrence
_____ 06697-4 TWILIGHT EMBRACE #86 Jennifer Rose
_____ 06698-2 QUEEN OF HEARTS #87 Lucia Curzon
_____ 06850-0 PASSION'S SONG #88 Johanna Phillips
_____ 06851-9 A MAN'S PERSUASION #89 Katherine Granger
_____ 06852-7 FORBIDDEN RAPTURE #90 Kate Nevins
_____ 06853-5 THIS WILD HEART #91 Margarett McKean
_____ 06854-3 SPLENDID SAVAGE #92 Zandra Colt
_____ 06855-1 THE EARL'S FANCY #93 Charlotte Hines
_____ 06858-6 BREATHLESS DAWN #94 Susanna Collins
_____ 06859-4 SWEET SURRENDER #95 Diana Mars
_____ 06860-8 GUARDED MOMENTS #96 Lynn Fairfax
_____ 06861-6 ECSTASY RECLAIMED #97 Brandy LaRue
_____ 06862-4 THE WIND'S EMBRACE #98 Melinda Harris
_____ 06863-2 THE FORGOTTEN BRIDE #99 Lillian Marsh

All of the above titles are $1.75 per copy

WHAT READERS SAY ABOUT
SECOND CHANCE AT LOVE BOOKS

"Your books are the greatest!"
—*M. N., Carteret, New Jersey**

"I have been reading romance novels for quite some time, but the SECOND CHANCE AT LOVE books are the most enjoyable."
—*P. R., Vicksburg, Mississippi**

"I enjoy SECOND CHANCE [AT LOVE] more than any books that I have read and I do read a lot."
—*J. R., Gretna, Louisiana**

"For years I've had my subscription in to Harlequin. Currently there is a series called Circle of Love, but you have them all beat."
—*C. B., Chicago, Illinois**

"I really think your books are exceptional . . . I read Harlequin and Silhouette and although I still like them, I'll buy your books over theirs. SECOND CHANCE [AT LOVE] is more interesting and holds your attention and imagination with a better story line . . ."
—*J. W., Flagstaff, Arizona**

"I've read many romances, but yours take the 'cake'!"
—*D. H., Bloomsburg, Pennsylvania**

"Have waited ten years for *good* romance books. Now I have them."
—*M. P., Jacksonville, Florida**

*Names and addresses available upon request